GIDEON'S VOW

HARTS OF THE WEST

SAMANTHA THOMAS

Thank you so much to Veronica G, and Christy C.
Your insight was invaluable.
An extra big thank you to Andrew G. for making this world so
much brighter for all of us.

1

———

Autumn Springs was bigger than she expected, but it was still the tiniest town she'd ever set foot in. With freshly painted wooden signs, and a board-walk swept free of the thick dust on the street; there was a civic pride that was apparent.

As the stagecoach approached the little town, it looked as if a meeting of buildings had taken place and plunked themselves down in the middle of nowhere. Mountains in one direction and trees in another. If one didn't know where to look, it would be nearly impossible to find.

It was perfect.

Taking a deep breath, Madeline thought to herself that this was the sort of place she needed, a place where no one would think to look for her and her brother. Her decision to come here, to this town over any other, was pure luck, but so far it was looking like the right one. A safe place with a sweet name.

Madeline glanced in Andrew's direction. Her young brother was swinging around one of the wood columns outside the stagecoach station, far less concerned of the dramatic turn their lives had taken. As he peeked around the wood, squinting and grinning at her with his infectious smile, she was reminded of why she had chosen to run. It was the right decision, for a number of reasons, but the enormity of the challenge that lay before her was starting to sink in. With the immediate danger gone, her bravery was beginning to wane.

Brushing a hand against her reticule, Madeline reminded herself that she had a finite amount of coin to get them both through the next several days. She had tucked away the last of her pin money prior to their parents' deaths and hadn't received another penny since her uncle had taken over their trust. It wasn't much, but it was all they had, and it would have to do. Every step since the moment she'd hidden them away on the train, had been a new experience, not all pleasant, but that didn't matter. She would find a way; she didn't have a choice. They needed a place to stay, and she needed employment. She'd never engaged a room in a hotel before, and she had certainly never worked a day in her life. Not paid work anyway. This was another reminder of the life she had left behind.

Deciding it was time for action, before she lost the last of her nerve, Madeline picked up the heavy valise she shared with her brother and readied herself. Before she had taken a single step, a streak of fur came barreling towards her, barely missing her legs and launching itself at Andrew. She gasped as her brother was knocked flat on his back. Expecting screams of terror, she was taken by surprise when she heard him laughing with each lick the friendly dog gave him.

A shout from the same direction the dog had come from, caught her attention. "Bandit, you wily cur! I told you to stay in the wagon!"

Madeline turned. She was surprised to see the voice had originated from the most angelic face she'd ever seen, surrounded by a tangle of blonde hair.

Andrew didn't seem hurt by the dog's enthusiasm, and Madeline stepped back as the child helped him to his feet, her little hands wiping away the dust on his jacket.

"Sorry, he's a bad listener, but I think he likes you. A lot."

The child was younger than Andrew, but nearly the same height. Her brother had always been small for his age. Ignoring any age difference or lack of acquaintance, this talkative creature didn't skip a beat.

"I never seen you here before."

In true Andrew form, instead of answering, he cocked his head to the side and asked a question of his own.

"You a girl?"

"'Course I am. My name's Tilly!"

Madeline was horrified at the indelicate question, but the little girl didn't seem offended at all.

His eyes widened at her assertion. Madeline thought he would hold to her side; he was usually wary around strangers—with good cause—but he surprised her by staying put.

"Why are you wearing pants?" he asked, pointing at the girl's covered legs.

Madeline didn't miss the mischievous glint in the girl's eye as she responded. "Wouldn't be proper if I didn't."

Fighting to bite back a smile at the precocious response, Madeline watched while Andrew looked confused at the little girl's amusement. She couldn't recall anything in their upbringing that would have prepared them for such an introduction. Madeline wondered what kind of people had created such a gregarious child.

She didn't have to wait long. A tall, dark-haired beauty,

far along in the family way, waved at them as she toiled across the street.

"Tilly! That dog of yours needs to learn some manners." The woman made her way to the boardwalk and came to a stop before Madeline, extending a hand.

"No, he don't."

"Doesn't." Both Madeline and the woman responded in unison.

Madeline blushed. "My apologies. I spoke out of turn. It's not my place: a habit, I suppose."

The woman gave her a bright smile. "Any help is appreciated, thank you. I'm Emma Hayes. Now it's my turn to apologize for that rather rough welcome."

Madeline hesitated for a moment, then shook the woman's waiting hand. It seemed that there was more for her to get used to in a small town, a forthright greeting being one of them.

"How do you do, Mrs. Hayes. I'm Madeline Sheppard." Then she realized that she had given her real name. She didn't know if she should be hiding such details or not. Yet another reminder of the steep learning curve that was ahead of her. She wasn't exactly bred for life on the run.

"Are you visiting, or are you thinking of making Autumn Springs your home? I haven't seen you before, and there aren't many women who come out this way on their own."

Madeline was stunned. Never had she met a woman so forward. In Portland, no one would have dared to ask such questions of a stranger, yet somehow Mrs. Hayes managed to do so without seeming offensive. It didn't take Madeline long to gather that young Tilly was much like her mother. That golden hair must come from her father.

The woman must have seen the look of wonder on her face. She laughed.

"I'm sorry, you must forgive me." She rubbed a hand across her rounded belly. "I haven't been able to do much this past few weeks, and your arrival is the most interesting thing that's happened in a while."

Thoughts of anonymity slipped away, but Madeline found herself smiling despite her surprise. Emma Hayes was like no one Madeline ever met before, but somehow, she already knew she liked her.

She self-consciously brushed the dust from her skirts. "I'm afraid I must look a fright Mrs. Hayes. We've only just arrived, and it was a dusty trip."

"Always is. You won't even notice it after a while. And please, call me Emma. Is this your son?" asked Emma.

The quick turn in conversation had Madeline's head spinning. "Yes—No, I beg your pardon, Andrew is my brother."

Madeline watched Emma observe her daughter with Andrew. Chin up, she prepared herself for the inevitable questions. She'd spent years, day in and day out with Andrew, helping him learn to read, and communicate clearly. He had already surpassed many of the limits others placed on him. She was so proud of him, he was a wonder, but Madeline knew whether in Portland or this Autumn Springs, people could be judgemental. No place was exempt from ignorance. She shouldn't expect this pretty little town to be any different. But Madeline didn't care what people had to say, only that her brother was safe.

But Emma turned back to her with a friendly chuckle. "Your brother's looking overwhelmed by Tilly. She can be a force of nature, but she has a heart of gold."

Madeline looked to see Andrew still wide-eyed as Tilly nattered on at a mile a minute, unfazed by the fact he was only responding to about half of what she said. The only thing that mattered to Madeline was that he didn't look nervous anymore. The last several months with their uncle had been awful.

"She's very friendly," agreed Madeline.

Emma laughed out loud.

"That is a very polite way of putting it."

Madeline blushed and decided a change of topic might be necessary.

"Do you know where I might find accommodations? Our stagecoach driver, Miss Quinn, mentioned there were a few options in town, but I must confess that I don't even know where to start looking."

"It won't take you long to get the lay of the land. Autumn Springs is growing quickly, but it's nothing like ... where did you say you're from?"

"Portland." Madeline snapped her mouth shut, but it was too late. In less than a span of five minutes, Emma Hayes had managed to get more information out of her than she'd given anyone since leaving the city.

Emma's eyes twinkled as she replied. "My husband is the sheriff here in Autumn Springs. He says my insatiable curiosity is only helpful half of the time."

The sheriff!

Madeline didn't know why the mention would give her pause. It wasn't as though she and Andrew were criminals. Running away from someone was not the same as running from the authorities. All the same, she needed to cut short this conversation.

"Forgive me, it's been a long trip. Those accommodations you mentioned?" asked Madeline.

"There is the International Hotel, if you are feeling fancy, and there are also quite a few boarding houses in town. I recommend Mrs. Durnford's. It's the next street over." Emma flicked a finger, indicating the direction.

"She's about to become Mrs. Wyley, but that won't affect the quality of the accommodations one bit. Along with two other ladies, she has been running it for some time. You'll want to stay away from the south of town. The saloons there might have rooms, but they're no place for a lady such as yourself, or your young gentleman brother. Many folks would prefer not to have them here, but it's still a mining town, and it unfortunately comes with the territory."

At the mention of the saloons Madeline gave a little shiver. It was a reminder that she was in a different type of place, and that she would need to figure out her next step as soon as possible. She planned to telegraph her father's old barrister in a few weeks, in the chance that he might be able to transfer some of her funds. The fact that her uncle was holding all the purse strings to her trust seemed entirely unfair, and she was hoping the barrister might be able to help.

"Thank you. I think I will try the boarding house you've recommended," said Madeline.

Emma gave her protruding stomach another rub and tilted her head at Madeline. "Are you sure I can't help you with anything else? I don't mean to be rude, but you do seem a little like a duck out of water."

This woman had no idea just how true that was. "We are fine. Thank you for your concern," said Madeline, hoping her tone conveyed an assurance she did not feel.

Emma was undeterred. "I know we've just met, but if there is something I can help with, please let me know. My family has been in these parts for quite some time. You've bumped into the right woman." She grinned, "Or should I say, we bumped into you."

For a moment, Madeline had the urge to spill all the fear and heartbreak of their last few weeks to Emma. She seemed to be genuine in her concern, and Madeline felt so very alone. Then good sense returned.

"Thank you. Your help with the accommodation is very kind and quite enough. Perhaps once I've secured myself some employment, we might meet again for a cup of tea."

Thinking that would be the end of the conversation, Madeline was surprised yet again when Emma replied.

"That would be wonderful! Then, you can meet my best friend, Nora. She's married to one of my brothers, you'll love her. Wait ... employment? You're looking for a job? What kind of work do you do?"

What kind of work did *she do*? That was a very good question. The truth was that through her time at Miss Alcott's Finishing School, and with her governess at home, she hadn't been trained toward any useful compensable employment. At least not in a place like this. Musical talents, hosting abilities, embroidery, and a passion for books didn't exactly translate into a paying job in a little mining town.

"Well, I ... I—"

"Tilly! Emma!"

From across the street came a deep booming voice. It belonged to an exceptionally tall, square-jawed, dark-haired man, standing next to a wagon full of supplies. His long legs were wrapped in wool trousers, melded to him as though they were a custom fit. The black vest he wore could not conceal the breadth of his chest. He cut a fine figure, but with his fist on his hips, standing on the hard-packed dirt, he mostly looked irritated.

"Daddy!"

The little girl ran across the street, jumping into her father's arms, Bandit close behind.

"Careful!" Emma cried out, as a passing wagon narrowly missed the hind legs of the dog.

Madeline glanced back over her shoulder to ensure that Andrew had no plans to follow. He remained on the boardwalk but was now looking rather dejected at the loss of the dog and the little girl.

"I won't keep you from your husband and daughter," said Madeline, trying to extricate herself from whatever this interaction was blossoming in to.

Emma's eyebrows shot skyward. "Husband?!" She made a good-hearted look of distaste and started to laugh. "Oh, heavens no. That's my brother Gideon. Tilly is my niece."

"Forgive me, I assumed. Proof that one should never make assumptions. I'm sorry."

Madeline felt foolish. The girl's light locks should have been enough of a clue. She gave a subtle glance in the man's direction. He scowled, except for the brief moment when he lifted his daughter into his arms, and his face lit up. Love for the child was written right across it. Once she was in the wagon, he gave the dog an annoyed glance and shook his head. The man had yet to smile at anything other than the little girl. Madeline found it hard to believe he was related to either Emma or Tilly.

As tired as she was, it was hard not to notice the man was as strong and handsome as any cowboy she'd read about, in the dime-store novels the girls used to secretly share at Miss Alcott's. Unfortunately, he didn't have the same friendly demeanor as his daughter and sister.

"Don't be. You couldn't know," said Emma.

"Your brother's wife must be lovely. Tilly's a beautiful child."

"Yes. She was," replied Emma, her tone almost dismissive.

Madeline was taken aback by Emma's comment. The child was a little disheveled, but in some strange way it added to her charm. If cleaned up even a little, the girl would be a picture of sweetness. Thankfully, Tilly wasn't in earshot of the unkind comment. Madeline was used to defending her brother, and now she felt the need to defend this child too.

"I think she's still lovely. Nothing a comb couldn't remedy."

Emma stared at her for a moment, then let out a roar of laughter. Everyone within hearing distance looked their way. Madeline felt her cheeks heat with the attention, but no matter how nice Emma Hayes had been to her, Madeline couldn't allow the child to be insulted in her presence. Madeline pushed back her shoulders and stood straightly.

"Oh, I think I like you very much, Madeline Sheppard. You're right, Tilly is absolutely beautiful, when she's clean. I was referring to her mother. Gideon's wife passed away, several years back. That's where those flaxen curls come from. All the rest of us Harts have dark hair."

If her cheeks were warm before, they positively flamed now. Madeline couldn't believe she had made such a rude assumption. She couldn't stand when others did it, yet here she was, making a most embarrassing one.

"I think I need to stop talking now. I believe my mind and my manners have left me somewhere on this journey."

"Please, don't apologize. I could never be offended by someone defending my niece. I admire your pluck."

"You're very generous," replied Madeline.

"Hmm." Emma tapped a finger to her chin. A gleam appeared in her eye. "You need employment, right? I think I might have a solution for you."

Not waiting for Madeline to respond, Emma picked up

her skirts and walked across to her brother and his wagon. She moved far quicker than Madeline expected from someone in her condition. Madeline watched as brother and sister spoke. A flurry of hands on Emma's part, and a determined shaking the head on his. Whatever was being discussed, it certainly wasn't in agreement. Madeline didn't need to overhear their words to know whatever impulsive idea Emma had come up with, it was not something her brother was entertaining.

Picking up her case she called to Andrew. "We need to go."

Andrew waved over to Tilly and gave her his bright smile, and the little girl waved back. It was the wave that distracted Emma from her debate.

"Don't go!" called Emma.

Madeline wasn't about to holler back across the street, no matter how relaxed societal norms might be in Autumn Springs. There were limits.

Giving the man a glare over her shoulder, Emma waddled back across the street.

"I need a little more time. You go on to Mrs. Durnford's. I'll be by in a little while."

"Please, don't cause a fuss with your brother. We will be fine. I can manage on my own."

Emma waved a hand as though brushing away Madeline's words. "Don't you worry. You'll make a perfect governess. I will meet you at Mrs. Durnford's this afternoon."

Governess!

There wasn't even time to protest, as once again, Emma sailed off. She left Madeline standing gaping on the boardwalk and made her way back to Gideon.

Flustered, Madeline decided it would be best if she and

Andrew left the depot station and the scene of heated sibling discussion. If they were lucky, Mrs. Durnford would have a room available for her and Andrew, and Emma Hayes would forget all about them. As friendly as she seemed, and as adorable as the young girl was, the last thing Madeline needed was to be in the employ of the world's grumpiest cowboy.

"No. Absolutely not."

Gideon glowered as he looked down at his little sister. If anyone thought that impending motherhood would cause her to quit her meddling ways, they would be sorely mistaken.

"You know I'm right. This is a perfect opportunity," said Emma.

"For who? Not for me, that's for sure," replied Gideon. "You need to mind your own business."

"And you need to think of Tilly."

Gideon looked over his shoulder at the smiling face of his daughter, being licked clean by her dog in the wagon. Just one look at her and his heart melted. Some days it felt like she was the only reason he kept going. Had she become slightly feral over the years with her mother gone? Maybe, but he'd never give voice to such thoughts, and he wouldn't put up with others voicing it either.

"Tilly's fine: she's happy." He gave his daughter a wink. "You happy, Tilly?"

"Yup, me and Bandit, we're happier than a—"

"That's fine." Gideon lifted his hand, stopping her from saying something that would only prove Emma's point.

Turning back to his sister, he could see by the 'told you so' look on her face, that he'd been too late.

"We all know she's happy. I'm not asking you to hire a playmate. You're doing a great job, Gideon. You're a good father—"

"I am. That girl is everything to me."

"Yes, but she needs a—"

"Don't. Don't you dare say 'mother.'" Gideon lowered his voice, but the last word still came out as a growl. "She gets all the love she needs from us."

"I wasn't going to say ... that. I was trying to say she needs a little feminine refinement. No matter how you slice it, that's something you and the boys can't provide. And since you haven't been willing to hire extra help for Teresa, Tilly hardly ever sees another woman. With me living in town, and a little one soon to arrive, you need help."

Gideon sighed. He hated when she was right. What might have been cute or even endearing when Tilly was smaller was not going to carry through as she got older. Emma wasn't wrong. Guidance was needed, but her suggestion was ludicrous.

He looked across to the woman his sister was referring to. She was a beauty, that much was obvious. But covered with silk, lace and a bewildered look on her face, Gideon doubted the woman had a clue what his sister was up to. And that boy with her, dressed like a tiny version of a banker, with his fancy suit and shoes? Neither one of them would last a week here.

He released a long low breath and stared down at his sister.

"Even if I was to consider hiring a governess for Tilly, why on earth would I chose some stranger who quite literally just arrived in town? And one that comes with a child?"

"Her brother."

"Whatever. We don't know anything about her. There can't be any good reason a lady like that has ended up in a place like this."

"'A place like this'? Autumn Springs is a wonderful town, a respectable town. And, while I don't know her entire story, I do know I like her."

Gideon scoffed. "You *like* her? Does she have references, experience, anything other than a pretty face to recommend her?"

Emma grinned at him. "You think she's pretty?"

Rolling his eyes, he responded. "How is that all you took from everything I just said?" He took a deep breath before continuing. "My point, dear sister, is that what she looks like doesn't equate to capability. Just look at her. I doubt she's even carried a bucket of water in her life."

"That's a rather presumptuous statement, and totally irrelevant. Tilly doesn't need to be taught how to do chores; she needs to be taught everything else. Miss Sheppard would be a perfect fit. Being around a lady like that would be a wonderful influence. I can see it now. You boys are so against the idea of mail-order brides, but how about a mail-order governess? But instead of waiting for one to arrive, you have one right here on your doorstep. Sounds down-right fortuitous if you ask me."

"No one's asking you."

Emma ignored this and kept talking. "I know that despite being a smart man, in this subject you are incapable of seeing reason."

"I know what you're up to," growled Gideon. "And you're meddling."

"If you mean, trying to find a way to help my open-minded, eldest brother, and assist a damsel in distress, then yes, you've caught me."

"Damsels that look like that are never in distress. They always find a way; it's in their nature," said Gideon.

"What a horrible thing to say! Honestly, Gideon. I know you're still having difficulty with losing Cordelia, but this awful attitude isn't helping anyone. If you won't help yourself, perhaps consider pushing aside your selfishness to help Tilly."

Emma's words stung with their truth. Gideon wondered again, if his family would be more understanding if they knew the truth. It wasn't worth the risk; he could never let Tilly know. He wasn't still grieving for Cordelia; he was living with the aftermath of her betrayal. But that was his burden to bear, not his child's. His family could think what they wanted; he wasn't going to change their minds with the truth. He had vowed that secret would remain his and his alone.

"How do you know she'd even contemplate working for me? You know nothing about the woman, or her brother. If she's such a lady, I can't see her stooping to take the job."

"But you'll consider offering it?" Emma pushed.

Gideon paused.

Perhaps he was approaching this all wrong. Instead of fighting with his sister about the woman, he could simply let the lady herself turn the offer down. The last thing some fragile city mouse wanted was to be working on a ranch outside of town. Despite Emma's belief that the woman would be grateful for the opportunity, Gideon knew her type. She would be horrified at the suggestion and, if he was lucky, she and her brother would be on the next stage out of town. Then, he would have done the right thing by offering to help her, his sister wouldn't be mad, at least not at him this time, and Gideon wouldn't have to have the prettiest woman he'd seen in years, wandering all over his ranch, disturbing his peace. The Double H would be left as it was, running smooth and woman free.

Certain he had managed to find the perfect answer to the problem before him, he smiled down at his sister. "Yes, I'll ask her. You're right."

Emma's mouth opened and then quickly shut, when she realized what he'd said. Gideon felt some small satisfaction in shocking his sister for once. Usually, it was the other way around.

"I'm right?" she asked.

"Yup."

"You're going to offer Miss Madeline Sheppard a governess position for Tilly ... at the Double H?" she confirmed.

Gideon had to suck in his cheeks to keep from smiling at Emma's incredulous look. He'd forgotten how much fun it could be to tease his sister.

"Yes. I am. You were very convincing."

Emma squeezed one eye shut as she considered him. "I don't know what you're thinking right now, but I'll take you at your word, that you'll ask Miss Sheppard. This is important, Gideon. I don't know why, but I get a feeling that they need the help. This solution could be beneficial for both of you."

"You have my word that I'll ask." He smiled as he promised her, hoping she wouldn't cotton to the way he worded his response.

A smile flashed across Emma's face, and she squeezed his fingers. "I'd hug you, if I could reach you." She chuckled ruefully as she rubbed a hand across her belly. "Thank you, Gideon. I've been feeling awful that I don't have the time for

Tilly that I once did. Miss Sheppard seems really nice, and her brother seems sweet as well. Tilly's already made him a friend. I have a good feeling about this."

"You got all that, from a few moments of conversation?"

"Yes."

"That you have a good feeling about this, reassures me less than you might think."

His sister turned her eyes heavenward. "Oh, stop. You're doing the right thing. I know things haven't been easy for you the past several years. You have a lot on your shoulders, but maybe Miss Sheppard will be able to help reduce that burden. You deserve that."

Watching the hypnotic sway of the afore-mentioned Miss Sheppard's skirts, as she rounded the corner of the boardwalk towards Mrs. Durnford's, Gideon gave a quick prayer that his plan would work. There was no way that having a woman like that around the Double H was going to make his days easier. Miss Madeline Sheppard was the last thing he needed in his life.

2

———

She had never felt so grateful for a glass of cold tea. It was the perfect combination of tart and sweet, and exactly what she needed after the long trip into Autumn Springs. Mrs. Durnford had the refreshment ready before Madeline had even had a chance to take their case inside. It was as though she knew what was needed first.

Sitting on the porch outside the rooming house, Madeline watched Mrs. Durnford smile affectionately at Andrew as he finished his second glass of the treat, with much relish. She had to stifle her sigh of relief before it became vocal.

Emma Hayes had been correct in her recommendation of the boarding house. Both Madeline and Andrew had been welcomed in as if they were family, not recent strangers to town. If Mrs. Durnford noticed anything about Andrew's appearance that differed from others, she never said a word. She simply ushered them in and made them feel at home. From the embroidered hangings on the wall, to her treatment of Andrew, Madeline could surmise she was a godly woman, and with each moment that passed Mrs. Durnford was proving that she lived her faith, not just preaching it. That wasn't always the case, and Madeline felt herself immensely relieved.

"So, you're from Portland," said Mrs. Durnford.

"Yes." On the walk over to the boarding house Madeline had decided that honesty would be the best policy. If she hoped to make a home here, she didn't want to alienate the people who lived here with deception. "This is my first time outside of Oregon. Andrew's, too."

"We're on an ad- ad-venture," added Andrew.

"We are," nodded Madeline. She turned back to the older woman, again thankful that she didn't seem put out by Andrew's interruption. "Thank you again, for having us here. And also, for this wonderful tea. I don't think I've ever had anything so delicious."

Mrs. Durnford beamed at the compliment. "Well, thank you. I'll confess it's not difficult to make, and a bit of honey seems to be the trick. The doctor's wife has a hive right here in town, so we are lucky to have a fresh supply nearby. That's Nora Hart. You mentioned that you've met Emma already, so I expect that Nora won't be far behind. Those girls have been friends since childhood, and since Nora married one of Emma's brothers, they've also become sisters."

"One of her brothers? I briefly saw one brother, I believe it was Gideon, earlier. I didn't realize there were more." Madeline wondered just how many there were. Perhaps that was where Emma gained such shocking confidence.

Mrs. Durnford gave a chuckle, and her ample bosom shook. "Oh yes, five in total. You can't miss them when you see them. Each one as tall as the pines, and with good character to the last man. Poor fellows can hardly walk down the street without the local matrons throwing their daughters in their paths. With only Micah married, it gives the local ladies hope."

"That actually sounds quite awful," said Madeline. "For the Harts, I mean."

"That's life in Autumn Springs," smiled Mrs. Durnford.

Portland wasn't much different. A decent prospect for an advantageous marriage wasn't always easy to find, for man or woman. Never mind if you had six children to find matches for. Madeline couldn't imagine having five brothers. She had always had her hands full with only one. Although she was sure it had been a busy childhood, there was still something wonderful in the idea of a large family. To never feel alone. Maybe if she had an older sister or brother, they wouldn't be in this situation now. Madeline sighed inwardly. There was no point in wishing for what wasn't.

"Speaking of Harts," Mrs. Durnford focused behind Madeline with an amused look.

Madeline turned in her seat to see Emma approaching the house. How the woman was able to traipse about town in her condition was astounding to Madeline, and even more so, that she wore a bright smile while doing so.

Andrew gave a shout of glee when he saw Tilly and forgetting any manners, he ran down to meet her. Madeline was amazed by the sudden change in her normally shy brother. The two were immediately caught up looking for 'good' rocks, on the carriageway beside the house, and Emma made her way to the ladies.

"Madeline, Mrs. Durnford! I'm so glad you found each other."

Madeline stood up and offered Emma a hand as she ascended the stairs to the porch.

"Thank you. I'm not quite as nimble these days," said Emma.

"You should be at home resting, you don't want that child arriving early," cautioned Mrs. Durnford.

Emma smoothed her hand over her belly as she lowered herself into the chair that Madeline had been sitting in. "I hope you don't mind, it's the closest one." She smiled as she indicated the chair she'd just taken.

"Not at all," replied Madeline, as in turn she took Andrew's vacated seat.

"Oh, don't you worry, Mrs. Durnford. I've already had a chat with this baby. We've agreed that it must wait until after your wedding to make an appearance. I have no intentions of missing the festivities."

"I think your husband just wants to confirm in person that my Jasper is married off, and no longer underfoot," laughed Mrs. Durnford.

"I'll only admit that we will all be happy when you've both spoken your 'I do's'. Your intended is becoming quite the worrywart, thinking you might still change your mind," said Emma.

"I like to keep him on his toes. It's good for him."

Emma and Mrs. Durnford joined in laughter, and Madeline couldn't help the giggle that bubbled up in her. Who were these people, who were so comfortable with who they were and each other? She couldn't help but feel a twinge of envy at their easy manner with one another. Would she ever fit in with people like this, in a place like Autumn Springs?

Emma turned to her.

"Miss Sheppard! Madeline, I have wonderful news for you. And as such, it warms my heart to see your brother and Tilly getting along so well. Once Gideon's done in town, he will come by. He's very excited to offer you the position of governess for Tilly."

From what Madeline observed earlier, she was certain that excitement was definitely not the emotion Emma's brother was feeling.

"Governess? I don't know what to say. I appreciate your efforts, but I don't believe I have the qualifications for such a position."

"Of course, you do. It's not as though it's a job at some finishing school. It's one child, who needs to be taught some refinement. That's all," said Emma reassuringly.

"That's a wonderful idea," chimed in Mrs. Durnford. "Gideon is a kind, fair man, and this would be a wonderful situation for you and Andrew. The Double H will be a wonderful experience for your brother."

"There. You see!" grinned Emma.

"I don't know," Madeline hesitated as she tried to wrap her mind around the idea of working as a governess to that sweet little girl. She didn't have a lot of employable skills, but Madeline had been the one to take on Andrew's education when her parents had called her back from school to help them out. Guiding Andrew through his challenges had been difficult at times, but he had already shown how capable he was, when given a chance. It had taken perseverance on both their ends, but they were getting there. He had also taught her many things a person couldn't learn through a book.

"I've never worked as a governess before," said Madeline.

"I never ran a boarding house, until I did," Mrs. Durnford replied. "Proverbs 19:21, 'Many are the plans in a person's heart, but it is the Lord's purpose that prevails.'"

Madeline felt the prick of tears threaten to fall. These

two women had shown her more compassion and friendship than she'd expected. Certainly, more than she'd recently experienced. The pressures of the past several weeks came crashing down.

"I didn't really have a plan." Madeline quickly brushed away an escaping tear.

Emma spoke softly. "You don't have tell us a thing. But I do know that you would be safe with my brother, at our family home. My other brothers are there too. If safety is a concern, please take my word that you will have it with my family."

Again, Madeline was at a loss for words. After a lifetime of so many decisions being made for her, it was hard to know who to trust, and what to do in every new situation. For what it was worth, Madeline's instincts told her these people did not mean them harm.

"I'm sorry, you've only just met me, and you must think me a watering pot. I promise I'm not usually one for so many tears." Madeline wiped away the wet streaks from her cheeks.

Emma waved away Madeline's words. "Not at all. I think I've cried more over the past few months than I have in my entire life, but that doesn't make me a weaker woman."

"Why the tears, Miss Sheppard?" asked Mrs. Durnford.

Madeline didn't even know where to begin.

"I'm not quite sure what I've done. I only know that I had to do it. I had to protect Andrew."

The dam now broken, Madeline told the two women about the death of her parents, her uncle August taking over her family estate, and his awful intention of sending first Andrew, then her, to the Oregon Hospital for the Insane, guaranteeing he had full control of all their parents' affairs.

"I tried to convince him it wasn't necessary. That I

could continue to care for Andrew; it would require nothing from him. I showed him research Father had had sent over, from a doctor in England named John Langdon Down. He had shown that patients just like Andrew could live a full life, one of happiness and dignity. But Uncle August wouldn't even consider it. He wanted Andrew shut away, and he said if I didn't agree, he would have me committed as well. He explained how easy it would be. His friend was the superintendent there. Proof wasn't necessary: the word of a man was more than enough to have a wife committed, never mind a niece. He warned me that it would be easier for him with Andrew and I out of sight. That if I fought him, he would lock both of us away."

Neither woman responded, but Madeline could see the outrage in their eyes matching the one in her belly as she spoke.

"I couldn't allow that to happen. I pretended to agree to my uncle's terms, on the understanding that I would be the one to take Andrew to that awful hospital; that I be allowed to say goodbye. Uncle August's arrogance allowed him to be so pleased with my acquiescence that he never suspected a thing. I'm sure he hoped that with one ward out of the way, it would easier to dispense with the other. On the day I was to deliver Andrew, I packed what I could of our things in one case, and my brother and I left on the first train out of Portland. That eventually took us to Butte, and once there, for lack of a better plan, I chose the stage out to the town with the friendliest-sounding name."

"Autumn Springs," murmured Emma.

"Yes, Autumn Springs," nodded Madeline. "I was fortunate that Miss Quinn was driving. She promised to forget she had ever seen us, if anyone came asking. She's a most unusual character, but she has a generous and understanding heart."

"Quinn is good people. What a journey it's been, you poor things." Mrs. Durnford reached to pat her hand. "Don't you worry. You have us now; we will figure things out."

Madeline nodded. "I believe I will. It will just take some adjustment. I'm not usually one to back down from a challenge, although I fear the past few weeks have certainly put that statement to the test."

"I believe you will, too," agreed Emma. "I have a really good feeling about this."

Mrs. Durnford tilted her head as she looked over to Madeline. "You know, if you're so inclined, I can bet there'd be a line of gentlemen here in Autumn Springs who would be overjoyed to have a wife as lovely as you. And not just the miners. I can name several well-suited men right now. There's Sam Matthews who owns the International Hotel, and James Fitzpatrick, who own one of the mining companies. Emma here could attest to their character."

Madeline noticed the frown on Emma's face. "I don't think we need to push matrimony on Madeline quite yet. As you've heard, I have already come up with a solution, Mrs. Durnford. I'm sure you can see the long-term value in that?"

"I was only saying—"

"That this is likely the best idea for *both* Gideon and Madeline. You're so right." Emma gave both women a bright smile.

Madeline thought it best to interject. "I'll confess that I entertained the idea of a husband and family of my own one day, but circumstances have changed. It's not just me that comes to a marriage." She indicated discreetly toward her brother. "Having a sibling along might not be as appealing, to some men."

She left out the fact that word of her inheritance also brought out the worst in men. They would do and say almost anything to get their hands on it.

Mrs. Durnford cleared her throat. "I'm not one to mince words, my dear, and I believe you may be correct in assuming such, but there is something else you need to keep in mind."

"What's that?" asked Madeline.

"The man that does open his home and his heart to the both of you will be the best of the lot. Don't settle. I was guilty of that in the past, myself. Only now, in these later years am I seeing what blessings a true man of character can bring to a home. It's a lesson I hope you learn now."

"Sage advice, Mrs. Durnford, and I am sure you can see why the brilliant solution I have found makes so much sense," said Emma.

Madeline didn't miss the pointed look Emma gave the older woman and was reminded of one of her favorite books by Jane Austen, whose main character carried the same name as her new friend. If Emma Hayes had any thoughts of playing matchmaker, Madeline could only assume it was for one of her other brothers, and not Tilly's father. Gideon Hart might be a fine-looking man, but he had the demeanor of one who would rather shoot Cupid down, than be party to any sibling matchmaking.

Which was just fine with Madeline. Her only hope was to find suitable employment to provide for herself and Andrew, until she could sort things out with her father's barrister. Once that was done, they would be fine. She would see to it.

The idea of working on a ranch was rather daunting, and Madeline realized that she might not have the appropriate attire.

"I don't know. Is there a shop nearby that might supply some ranch clothing?"

Madeline wasn't sure how far she could stretch the little money she had, but hopefully it would be enough to outfit Andrew and herself accordingly.

"Ranch clothing?" Emma's snort of laughter made Madeline realize that she must have said something ridiculous.

"Even Gideon won't expect a governess to work as a ranch hand. What you have is just fine. I can also find a few of my dresses that might fit, if you don't mind. You're a bit smaller than I am, particularly now," said Emma, as she rubbed her rounded belly. "A little nip and tuck here and there so you aren't tripping over your skirts, and you'll be ready to go."

"Thank you, Emma. I don't know what to say. I don't think I've ever met anyone so generous."

Emma swiped at the air, pushing away Madeline's words. "You're helping my family, it's the least I can do. As for your brother, he's a fair bit smaller than my brothers were, but I'm sure that something will work."

"He's shorter than some for his age, but that does not reflect his capability."

Emma's eyes widened at the subtle reprimand. "Why ever would it?"

Madeline blushed, realizing her error. "I'm so sorry. I seem to be inclined to misinterpret your words ... again. You have been nothing but kind and gracious to me from the moment we met. I think you'll find that I'm rather protective of my brother."

Apparently satisfied that she had not offended, Emma responded. "Nothing wrong with that, he's your family. I only hope in time you'll realize that you won't have to worry about those kinds of things here. Not at the Double H anyway."

"Thank you. Both of you." Madeline smiled at Mrs. Durnford.

"Don't thank us yet. While you might be trying to teach Tilly to engage in more ladylike activities, I fear your gentleman brother will also be learning a few new things." Emma nodded in the direction of the children.

Madeline turned around to witness Tilly giving Andrew a lesson in the fine art of spitting. Her brother did his best to follow her directions.

"Oh, heavens," sighed Madeline.

"As I was saying," laughed Emma.

Turning her back to the children, she gave Emma a smile. "I can't say I approve, but as long as he is safe and happy, I think I can accept that he will acquire some new habits."

Mrs. Durnford didn't seem overly impressed, but even she was forced to join in the laughter when Andrew finally succeeded in getting Tilly's approval.

It was all so different than what she was used to, but if Emma's brother truly wanted a governess for his daughter, then she would take the position once offered. Tilly appeared to be a wonderful, if energetic child, and while Madeline was hesitant to work for an unfamiliar man, she hoped that between Mrs. Durnford's recommendations and Emma's assurances, both she and Andrew would be safe under his employment. Madeline would have had to be blind not to see why ladies in town might swoon over Mr. Hart, but an awareness of the man's physical attributes would not change her behavior. If they agreed on the posi-tion, then he would be her employer, not her friend, and perhaps that distinction was for the best.

Working for the stern Gideon Hart, she certainly wouldn't have to worry about any complications with tenderness or affection. Any relationship they had would be professional, nothing more. Exactly what was needed.

HE'D ONLY COME into town to get a few supplies, not add two more mouths to feed at the Double H. Especially when one mouth came attached to a lady as pretty as Miss Sheppard. Gideon shook his head, as he made his way with the team down Main Street. Emma definitely had match-making on the mind, but she would realize soon enough, that there was never going to be another city gal that turned his head. Ever. Things were fine the way they were. Wife free.

Gideon drove the wagon around the corner to the boarding house and saw the three ladies on the porch with Tilly and the boy playing nearby. It did his heart good to see her so happy. Knowing his daughter was happy, safe, and loved was all he cared about.

From the corner of his eye, he noticed the owner of Belle's Palace, Floyd Keller, making his way along the boardwalk from the south of town. Not bothering to remove the toothpick from his mouth, he grinned at Gideon with a slow dip of his chin. Keller was straying from his haven of sharp-shooters and card sharks, and Gideon didn't like it. There was no lost love between the two men, since the trouble his brother Ben got into two summers past, but for the most part it was easy to avoid Floyd altogether.

When Gideon pulled up to Mrs. Durnford's, Keller was leaning against the side of the building across the street. His gaze was clearly on the ladies enjoying their tea, and Gideon had a feeling the saloon owner's interest wasn't in the old

Sheriff's intended or his sister. He had the look of a man appraising cattle for purchase, and Gideon's blood grew hot.

Unexpected irritation propelled him from the wagon, and ignoring the welcome from Emma and Tilly, he stomped across the dusty street and stepped in close to Keller, forcing the man's back against the wooden wall.

"You got business here, Keller? Because I don't think you do." Gideon kept his voice low. He could smell the spirits on Keller's breath.

Rolling the toothpick across his bottom lip, Keller gave a slow insolent smile. "Don't see how that's any business of yours, if I do. 'Lessen you're afraid of a little competition."

"There's no competition here." It was a statement, but the warning was clear.

"Why's that? You think you Harts get first crack at every new skirt that arrives in town? I don't think so, *Gideon*." The man uttered his name as though it was an insult.

"Most times I've got no interest in what you're up to but let me be clear about this. You so much as speak to that young lady over there, and you and I are going to have a quarrel. After last time, I'd think you'd know better than to try me."

The man raised his hands in supplication. "Fine, fine. Take it easy there, big fella. Though I can't see the big deal."

"You heard me," growled Gideon.

"I did," said Keller as he slunk away from Gideon. A little farther down the boardwalk back to the south of town, he tossed his final words over his shoulder. "Tell Benny-boy that we miss him at the tables." He chortled as he retreated towards his part of town.

Gideon's fist clenched, and he reminded himself to breathe. Whatever the fool said meant nothing if he heeded Gideon's words and kept his distance.

Turning his attention back to the boarding house, he saw all three women standing, as though waiting for some disaster to strike. At least the children hadn't noticed. It wasn't the best way to make a first impression, but there was nothing to be done about that now. Not that he should be concerned what this woman thought of him anyway. She was going to be his employee, not his wife, he would keep her safe his way and on his own terms.

Wife? Employee. If she accepted the offer. Where had that thought come from? His hope was for her to *not* accept his offer.

He certainly had no desire to wed the woman, but his plan to avoid his sister's machinations had suddenly flown out the window, with the vile saloon owner's leering gaze. She would have to agree to work for him. It was the only way to satisfy his sudden and inexplicable need to ensure her and the boy's safety.

He hadn't liked the way Keller was looking at Miss Sheppard, and Gideon knew there was something different about her brother. Knowing Floyd Keller as he did, if Miss Sheppard fell into his grasp, things wouldn't bode well for either one of them.

Foolish woman. What was she doing here anyway? He took a moment to eye the woman his sister seemed determined to foist on him. She looked every inch a lady, but hardly fit for life out here. And what use was that thing on her head? The modest brimmed hat was perched perfectly atop her head with a large pin pushed into a swirl of black hair. The Montana wind would make short work of that monstrosity soon enough. She was a duck out of water, and there were too many hunters around.

There was hardly anything to her. A good dust storm could blow her away. She didn't belong in a place like this, and neither did her little brother, all dressed up like he was some sort of businessman instead of a kid. Gideon couldn't even imagine having to wear clothes like that as a young boy. That costume wouldn't last long out here, the boy must be sweltering beneath the bright sun. He would need to remedy that for the kid immediately.

Gideon grunted and gave his head a shake. How he'd gone from *absolutely not*, to properly outfitting some kid he'd never met, was a mystery. He was even more irritated, knowing how pleased his sister would be. He wouldn't have put it past Emma to go and convince Keller to show up, just to get under his collar.

Well, he'd show her. He had no intentions of being anything other than a paycheck to this woman. Arm's length and unavailable, no matter what his sister planned.

With the saloon owner gone, Gideon walked over to greet the waiting ladies. Miss Sheppard was looking at him like he was some sort of rabble-rouser. Maybe where she came from men didn't threaten violence to protect those who couldn't defend themselves, but Gideon knew exactly who Floyd Keller was, and what he was capable of. He felt no shame and he wouldn't hesitate to do the same thing all over again. Whether this self-righteous city woman agreed or not.

"Thank you for removing the riff-raff, Gideon. Can I get you some tea?" offered Mrs. Durnford.

At least Mrs. Durnford had enough sense to know what was necessary.

"No, thank you, ma'am. While I appreciate the offer, I'm only here on business, and the sooner that's handled, the sooner I can get back to the Double H," replied Gideon.

"Wonderful!" Emma clapped her hands together. "Gideon, this is the lovely Miss Madeline Sheppard. As we discussed, she would be a perfect governess for Tilly. Or tutor, habit breaker, whatever title the two of you decide to call it."

Governess. It was such a stuffy word for someone who was simply teaching manners, and lady kinds of activities. All he really needed was a decent woman who didn't have marriage on the mind. *Governess.* Honestly, this woman looked more like the sort to be hiring one than acting as one. Still, his sister for all her meddling, wasn't usually wrong about people.

"It's nice to meet you, Miss Sheppard. My sister tells me that you are in need of employment, and that looking after my Tilly might be a good solution for us both."

"Thank you, Mr. Hart." The woman looked nervous. "I feel it's only fair to tell you that I have never been employed as a governess before and I have no references. I have, however, been almost solely responsible for my brother's education over the past several years, and I like to think that between Andrew's perseverance and my encouragement, he is where he is today."

Gideon cut his eyes over to Andrew as the boy played with Tilly and nodded. "I can see that." He turned back to Miss Sheppard. "You ever lived on a ranch, or even seen one before?"

"No. I have not."

"You ever have *any* kind of job?"

Her creamy pale cheeks pinkened, as she responded. "No, I have not."

"You look like you're more suited to the city." He paused, then added, "that's not an insult."

"It's doesn't sound like a compliment either, Mr. Hart."

He watched as the woman squared her shoulders at him. He felt a flicker of respect at her response. He had just discovered that she wasn't one to cower. That would serve her well out here.

Gideon could feel the searing heat of his sister's gaze, but Emma remained surprisingly silent, and he pressed on. "It's only an observation. You won't be responsible for chores, but as much as I love my home, the Double H doesn't have all the amenities you might be used to."

She lifted her chin high and steady blue eyes met his. "I like to believe that I am adaptable."

Her pride was evident, and Gideon had to admit she already had more fight in her than he had expected. Although he was impressed, he couldn't stop from pushing her further. How long could she keep her composure when riled?

"I'm not sure how long we'll need you. I can tell you it won't be permanent. Once we get a good teacher here in town, Tilly will be going to school with the other children. Then you'll have to find another position."

He didn't need to look at his sister to know that Emma was getting upset. He could feel her eyes boring into him. To her credit, Miss Sheppard didn't even flinch at his words.

"Are you still offering me a position, Mr. Hart?"

Hadn't he made himself clear? "Yes."

She just stood there. Narrowing her eyes, as if she were assessing *his* suitability for the job. Like she was the one doing *him* a favor. More proof that despite her apparent desperate circumstances, she was still another entitled woman from the city. Did he really need another one of those back on his land?

Emma cleared her throat, then spoke. "What do you think, Madeline? It seems like a good answer to your ... situation."

Gideon watched as the woman's shoulders drooped and

she sighed in response to Emma's words. Her *situation*? What was that all about? Was she some sort of criminal? He doubted that was the case, since Emma would never place Tilly in any kind of danger. Maybe it was best he didn't know. Arm's length, he reminded himself.

She was taking too long to decide, and he'd had enough. He wasn't leaving her here at the mercy of men like Keller, and there was work to be done at the Double H and he needed to get back to it.

"I don't know why you're hesitating. It sounds like you and your brother need a place to stay, and I've got a daughter who needs some teaching. I'm willing to pay and house you to do it. What more do you need to know?"

Miss Sheppard glanced back to Emma and Mrs. Durnford, as though she were looking for reassurance. Gideon knew his sister was angry with him, but she still smiled encouragingly at Miss Sheppard. Now he was certain Emma had matchmaking on her mind. Normally his sister would give him a dressing down for his behavior.

"Just think what a wonderful chance it will be for Andrew."

With the mention of her brother, both Gideon and Madeline turned to see Tilly and Andrew now sitting together in the wagon.

"Wonderful," muttered the flustered Miss Sheppard. Picking up her skirts, she marched toward her brother. "Andrew, get down from there," She issued her command in a hushed tone.

"Tilly says we are going home," replied Andrew, making absolutely no effort to move.

"It's not our home and that's not our wagon. Please remove yourself, Andrew."

Gideon took the chance to grab Miss Sheppard's case

before he joined her at the wagon and placed it in the back. "Boy's fine where he is." He looked over to the beaming Andrew. "Lot less stubborn than his sister."

Gideon had to hide the twitch of his lips as the two children giggled at his assessment of Miss Sheppard. She was looking at him like she might want to tear a strip right off him, and Gideon could now see where she might be effective at keeping at least the children in line.

"As much as I realize the generosity of your offer Mr. Hart, I have to say you are not making it very appealing." She spoke quietly, but Gideon noticed that although she was clutching the sides of her skirt, it did not stop the shaking of her hands. She was nervous, perhaps even scared, and rightfully so. Part of him wanted to reassure her, let her know he was no danger to her and her brother. Unfortunately, it was the other part of him, the one that thought she was making too much of a fuss over the whole thing, that spoke out.

"It's an offer of employment, Miss Sheppard. You're not picking out a new dress: it doesn't have to be pretty."

Her big blue eyes widened at his remark, and Gideon felt a pang of regret. He didn't know why he was being so ornery, around a woman who had done him no harm. Was it just because of her fancy outfit and the way she reminded him of Cordelia? Gideon knew he wasn't being fair, yet he couldn't stop himself. If any one of his brothers had heard how rude he was being, he would have felt more than disapproving looks on the back of his head.

"I'm sor—"

"Mr. Hart. I don't know what I have done to make you think so poorly of me, but perhaps I am not what you need."

"First off, let me be clear. It's not what I need: it's what my daughter needs."

Gideon took off his hat and ran his fingers through his thick, dark hair before putting it back on. "Now look, Miss Sheppard. I don't mean to be rude, and by the look on your face, you like this about as much as I do. But we both need help and for now, this seems to be the best solution."

He gestured with his chin over to where Floyd Keller was standing watching their interaction from down the street. "You have other choices, but I'd say, this would be as good a choice as any. Purely transactional. You and your brother will be safe at the Double H. You have my word that you will be under my protection."

Those big eyes nervously took in the Belle's Palace owner, then the two happy children in the wagon. She sighed. She kept him waiting a moment longer before she replied.

"Fine. I accept."

She thrust out her hand, and he took it in his to shake. Her covered hand seemed so small in his large, calloused one, and something kicked in his chest. He released her fingers immediately, not wanting to dwell on what had just happened.

He stepped aside and waited impatiently as Miss Sheppard, his new employee, said her goodbyes to Emma and Mrs. Durnford. She walked toward him, head high and back straight as a poker. As she reached the wagon, Gideon could see she was at a loss as to how she would get herself up to the wagon's bench. She was probably used to a private carriage over buckboards and buggies.

The devil suddenly took him, and Gideon quickly grabbed her by the waist and swung her up and on to the seat before she could let out a protest.

"Mr. Hart!" she gasped.

"Miss Sheppard," he replied. "I warned you we do things different out here."

It was an outright lie, and Gideon knew it. He enjoyed creating a wrinkle in that starched composure of hers. What was he thinking? What had possessed him to act so impetuously? As he settled himself in beside her on the bench, he didn't miss the amused face of Mrs. Durnford, and the smug smile on his sister.

Meddlers, the whole lot of them.

Making a short clicking noise, Gideon took his leave of the two smirking women on the boarding house porch. Two kids tucked in back, and one shocked stranger with her leg brushing against his. They were headed home, but somehow it felt a whole lot more like he was heading into trouble.

3

———————

Madeline quietly studied the brooding man next to her. He looked like a man who had been tempered by experience and bronzed by the sun. His hat was tipped so low over his eyes, that if she were a few inches taller, she would not be able to see them at all.

Not that she was attempting to gaze into them now. The man had been determinedly staring ahead since they left Autumn Springs, despite their close proximity, or perhaps because of it. Since he was deliberately avoiding eye contact, Madeline was able to surreptitiously scrutinize the mysterious Gideon Hart.

There was a day or two's growth of stubble that didn't quite hide his strong jawline. Madeline imagined it must have gotten that way from all the clenching he did. His long legs looked like they'd be more comfortable astride a horse then tucked into this wagon. He had thick hands, darkened by long hours working in the sun. They were so different from her father's and her uncle's. He wasn't even wearing gloves as he held the reins of his team in his fingers. They were the hands of a man who had known hard work, and in contrast to her own, she could almost forgive his dismissive presumptions of her. Almost.

The road, if one could even call it that, to the Double H ranch was well worn. Madeline managed to keep herself steady, but each time a wheel caught, her knee would brush against the muscled length of Mr. Hart's thigh, and his scowl would deepen. How anyone could hold such a hard look for so long was incredible to her. When Madeline was little, her governess used to tell her that her face would freeze that way if she sulked too long. It wasn't as though he wasn't capable of smiling; she had seen it when he looked at his daughter. If it was merely her presence that affected the man so, Madeline hoped that in time, his vexation with her would diminish.

If her brief time at Miss Alcott's Finishing School had taught her anything, it was how to appear calm in the face of adversity. Madeline had drawn from that teaching often over the past several weeks, and she would apply it now. If Mr. Hart knew how anxious she really was, he might rescind his offer, and she needed this position.

The truth was that Madeline was more than grateful for his assistance. She didn't know why she was letting his demeanor put her off. She had certainly dealt with far worse, in her uncle and his awful underlings. There was no telling when, or even if, she would receive funds or help from her father's barrister. She had briefly contemplated answering an ad to become a mail-order bride, but quickly dismissed the idea. There was no guarantee of how she and Andrew would be treated, and once she was wed, she would have even fewer options. A decision like that was leaving a lot up to chance, and Madeline didn't believe in gambling.

At least she hadn't until this decision.

Gideon Hart might not be the friendliest option, but he

was currently the least dangerous one. Although she had initially been shocked by his behavior with the saloon owner, she now saw that he was not a man to be trifled with. For the first time since her parents had passed, Madeline felt secure. He may not be thrilled with their arrangement, but he was kind to Andrew and Madeline was confident that in his employ, both she and Andrew would be protected.

Ignoring the discomfort of her stays digging into her hips with each rattle and bump of the wagon, she allowed a sigh of relief to escape.

His eyes cut in her direction at the sound. "Better get used to it. There are no city streets out this way."

He thought she was complaining.

Of course, he did. He probably took one look at her when he'd first seen her in Autumn Springs and written her off as useless. His mistake. His assumptions regarding her failings only gave her incentive to prove him wrong.

She wondered if he was as antagonistic with all the women in Autumn Springs. Madeline could only believe it was the other Hart brothers that had the ladies in town all in a tizzy, as Mrs. Durnford described. If Gideon Hart was included in their marriage ambitions, it proved the point that only men who were rich or handsome could get away with being so humorless. And Mr. Hart was a simple rancher.

Madeline was reminded how lucky she was to have avoided the path of mail-order bride. Imagine if she was married to a man like this, instead of employed. As an employee, she had the ability to walk away whenever she chose. She shook the thought from her mind. Mr. Hart's personality wasn't really a factor, if he treated her and her brother with respect. Anything thing else she could handle.

Mentally brushing away his words, she attempted a

more pleasant line of conversation. "It's nice to be away from the city, and even town. It's beautiful here. To be so close to the mountains is quite breathtaking. In Portland we can see Mount Hood on a clear day, but it's much different to be so close to them here."

There was a brief flicker of surprise in his eyes, before he looked away.

"It is."

She meant every word. The openness, so different from the city. In comparison, the tall buildings that loomed over the streets made it seem more like a prison. In some ways, it had been.

Determined to engage him, she tried again. "Have you always lived here?"

Mr. Hart sighed, and Madeline wondered if it was because he was realizing she wasn't going to give up. He might as well realize that now. She was far from a perfect person, but she was never one to quit.

"Most of my life."

"You're fortunate. It seems like a nice place to have grown up."

"It is. But it's not for everyone, though."

Ignoring his less than subtle dig, Madeline continued. "How much longer until we reach your Double H?"

"Well, it's not just mine, I've got three more brothers that have a stake in the ranch. You'll meet them soon enough. Then there's Micah, he's the doctor in town, and of course Emma, but she's married to Sheriff Hayes now. But in answer to your question, you've been on Hart land for the past half hour."

"Oh." It came out more as a whisper. For some reason, Madeline hadn't expected Gideon to be such a large land holder. "I had no idea. It's far more than I expected."

He didn't have the pretentious or grandiose air of the wealthy men she was accustomed to in the city. Looks like she was making assumptions too. Madeline realized there was going to be a steep learning curve for her when it came to Mr. Gideon Hart.

Noticing the corner of his mouth twitch at her astonished response before tamping down his amusement, Madeline was encouraged. His amusement was obviously at her expense, but it wasn't cruel and at least it was a start.

"With this much land, I can see why you are so busy. You've been so generous in helping Andrew and I, I'm hopeful that I will be able to remove one burden from your shoulders."

"My daughter isn't a burden. No child is." He kept his voice low, but his upset was clear.

"No! That's not what I meant at all. I only meant that I'm happy to help. I couldn't agree more, every child is a gift."

Madeline couldn't understand why he would jump to such an awful conclusion. Of course, she had done the same with his sister. Still, what on earth had made this man assume the worse of every word she spoke? The wariness in his eyes seemed to be solely directed at her. As they had only met mere hours ago, Madeline was having a hard time understanding what she had already done to make him so distrustful of her.

"I was only trying to say I am grateful, and I hope that you find some benefit in your kind offer."

Mr. Hart nodded, then narrowed his eyes before he turned them back to his team. "You aren't worried what folks might think, of a pretty young woman out at the ranch, alone, surrounded by men?"

Madeline wondered why her first thought wasn't to be offended by his words but instead surprise at his calling her pretty. She wondered if he even noticed he'd done so. To be fair, his question was a reasonable one to ask. If she had been offered this position even three months before, she would have turned it down immediately.

She looked behind to see Andrew and Tilly laughing as the dog joyfully licked faces while enjoying endless ear scratches.

"I imagine that wherever we go there will be talk. I believe if Andrew and I have been able to drown out gossip and speculation thus far, I don't see why I would start to pay it any heed now."

Mr. Hart grunted. Madeline couldn't tell if it was one of approval, but he appeared to accept her answer.

"I won't have you in the big house."

The man changed subjects as quickly as he changed his moods. Madeline suddenly had a vision of nestling down in a stall full of hay and wondered if accepting this job had been a rash decision.

Mr. Hart continued speaking before she could respond. "You can have my old—there's a cabin that is now sitting empty. It's close to the main house. It will afford you some privacy. You and your brother are welcome to it." He cleared his throat. "It will probably need some cleaning, no one has been there since ... well, all I'm saying is it might need a once-over with a broom or such."

He gave her another quick glance that made it seem as though he questioned her ability to even know how to use a broom.

"Thank you. I'm sure it will suit us just fine." Madeline meant every word. It didn't matter what shape the cabin Mr. Hart offered was in, as long as it was away from her uncle, and kept her and Andrew safe.

She took another breath, hoping to lighten the heaviness that sat in the pit of her stomach. Her emotions were all over. One moment relieved, the next, panic. Was she doing the right thing? Was this the safest plan of action she could be taking? Here she was, sitting next to a practical stranger, on the recommendation of two women she barely knew. Emma and Mrs. Durnford had assured her that Gideon Hart was a decent man, but what did Madeline know about the two women? She closed her eyes and tried to calm her racing heart.

As they travelled toward the Double H ranch, Madeline tried to focus on the magnificent view from the wagon seat. She wondered how everyone knew where they were going, with a nary a street sign to be seen. 'Head west' was such a vague guide, and so much looked the same. Hoping that Mr. Hart would not find offense in conversation surrounding trees and creeks she questioned him about the landscape.

Somewhat agreeable to the neutral topic, he began to point out landmarks, strange outcroppings and unusual trees. After a while she started to realize just how different each bend in the road really was, and she became determined to remember as much as possible so she would not feel like a lost babe in the woods.

"Thank you, Mr. Hart, it's quite a bit to take in but with such a beautiful classroom, I'm excited to learn." She hoped that her genuine appreciation for the land he called home came through.

"It's not always beautiful. We get wicked storms, and days so hot, and so cold that you wonder why you're here at all," he replied.

Not dissuaded by his rebuff, she continued. "I am looking forward to experiencing it all. I will embrace the chance of learning new skills and it will provide both

Andrew and I with a healthy dose of fresh air. *That* you certainly can't find in the city."

"Air's not always fresh when you're mucking out the stalls."

He gave her a brief satisfied grin, then turned back to the reins. Madeline was not to be undone by his negative response. She called on her patience and decided that she was going to kill Gideon Hart with kindness.

"I'm sure that only makes the air outside your barns that much sweeter."

"You got that right," mumbled Mr. Hart.

A voice from the back of the wagon piped up.

"Can I?"

She saw Gideon raise a brow as he glanced back at Andrew.

"Muck out stalls? Not sure you'd like that much, kid."

"Yeah, it smells real bad," chimed in Tilly.

"Horses don't smell." Andrew's lips pursed with indignation on behalf of the insulted animals.

"Yeah, they do" assured Tilly.

Hoping to prevent an argument, Madeline interrupted before her brother once again voiced his dissent.

"Andrew loves horses," she explained. "It's his current obsess ... interest. All things equine are wonderful to him. All things."

How on earth could she explain how Andrew tended to fixate on certain things? She didn't want to embarrass him by calling them obsessions, but the truth was that these days if anything was even remotely connected with horses, Andrew was interested. Madeline was lucky Andrew hadn't insisted on sitting up front with Mr. Hart, although her new employer may have preferred that.

"Well, I'm not doing it with you," declared Tilly. "I'll play with you after you wash up."

"Okay," replied Andrew.

Watching Mr. Hart's attempts to keep a straight face at the exchange nearly caused Madeline to let out a giggle. The man wasn't a complete block of ice after all.

"Neither of you need to worry about any of that. Let's get everyone settled before any chore lists are handed out," said Mr. Hart.

Madeline was surprised when Andrew remained quiet. He seemed content to accept anything Gideon had to say. Tilly, however, wasn't finished.

"I guess horses aren't too bad, but chickens?" Tilly paused to squeeze her nose and stick out her tongue in disgust. "I heard Lee Manning say chickens smell like a—"

"That's enough," barked Gideon.

The vivacious girl didn't look scared, but she did pause, seeming to momentarily obey her father's command. Then as the two children settled back down in the wagon, she held her hand to Andrew's ear, and loudly whispered, "I'll tell you later."

Madeline knew that if she had heard Tilly then so had her father. He didn't acknowledge it, but Madeline heard the deep sigh escape from his lips. Despite his abrasive demeanor she couldn't help but feel a little sorry for the poor man. Parenting couldn't be an easy task and dealing with the loss of his wife while trying to raise a precocious child was obviously becoming more than he could handle. It seemed that Emma was correct in her assessment of her brother's situation, and Madeline hoped she might be able to help the Harts as much as they were helping her.

Tilly was obviously intelligent, and certainly kind. She'd

just been left to learn a tad more than necessary from, what Madeline hoped, were the well-meaning men of the Hart ranch. Her personality was big and bright, and Madeline hoped that some of her unfailing confidence might rub off on Andrew. Neither Madeline or her brother had spent much time with people outside their household while their parents were still alive, and their world only became smaller once they resided with their uncle. It might be short-lived, but Madeline hoped they could make the best of the opportunities that their change of circumstances had provided them.

As Tilly chattered away in the back of the wagon with Andrew, Madeline allowed a comfortable silence to fall between herself and Mr. Hart. Listening to Tilly's vivid descriptions of the Double H ranch gave Madeline a far better idea of what to expect than she would ever get from the taciturn man beside her.

Praying they would soon find some common ground, Madeline sat quietly and prepared herself for the experience ahead.

GIDEON SNUCK at glance at the woman beside him, trying to assess what he'd gotten himself into. He'd be lying if he didn't admit that she was pretty as a picture, with the background of mountains and trees to frame her. Not that Gideon put much stock in such things. A beautiful face was no indication of a good heart. That was a lesson that he didn't need to be taught twice.

Her back was still as straight as the board she now sat on, but Gideon knew she had to be uncomfortable. When a woman chose fashion and appearance over practicality, she had no one to blame but herself. Gideon sighed inwardly, knowing Miss Sheppard hadn't earned such hostility.

He knew he was being uncharitable. She was likely as surprised to be here as he was. And the road really was worse than usual. After the last rain, the ruts in the road had gotten deeper and there were even a few moments where he thought Tilly and Andrew might be jostled right out of the wagon. Gideon wondered what the proper Miss Sheppard thought of her body pressing against his when her tight grip on the wooden bench wasn't enough to keep her balance. To her credit, she didn't utter one word of complaint. He grudgingly admired her efforts to be congenial and make conversation, although it was a waste of time. They were never going to be friends, she simply worked for him. He doubted they would have more than perfunctory conversation regarding Tilly's progress, once she was settled at the ranch.

Still, he couldn't help but wonder what kind of situation would have brought a woman like Miss Sheppard to Autumn Springs. All he knew was that she was from Portland. His sister had alluded to some sort of trouble but Gideon refused to ask Emma anything. Any interest he showed in Miss Sheppard, outside of Tilly's education, would only embolden his sister's match-making plans. She was probably already convinced of her success when he reflexively protected her from Floyd Keller. Emma should know better. Any decent man would have done the same.

This Miss Sheppard, with her heart-shaped face, hair darker than midnight, and that creamy complexion, she was strikingly beautiful, and there was no doubt she was going to become a target for the men of Autumn Springs. He didn't even want to think of the unscrupulous ones. Keller was already proof of that. She'd barely arrived and already they were swooping in. It didn't surprise him that word had spread so quickly through town. The woman had clearly lost her mind in coming here. She should have climbed right up on that stagecoach and gone back to where she came from. But she hadn't, and now he was responsible for her and her brother's safety. He needed to make sure she realized the severity of her situation.

"I don't want you going into town." said Gideon.

When he heard her sharp intake of breath, he realized it sounded like a demand, rather than concern.

"Am I to be a prisoner in your home, Mr. Hart?"

She gave him a nervous smile, trying to make light of it, but it was hard to miss the worry in her eyes. It was understandable. She didn't know him from Adam, and she had taken a giant leap of faith in agreeing to work for him.

"That's not what I meant. Just that it's best that you don't go into town alone."

"But I am permitted to go to Autumn Springs?"

"Of course. I meant by yourself." Why had this become difficult? Was she testing him? "But you should know that we don't go in every day."

He waited for a disappointed reaction. Instead, he was met with another calm smile. How could a woman, who had to be exhausted, maintain such a sunny disposition? Could she really be this pleasant all the time? If their roles were reversed and he were the teacher, he would have to give her an A for effort.

"I understand—oof!" Repositioning herself after another bump in the road, she continued. "I expect that I will be quite busy with my new responsibilities."

Gideon snuck a look back at the children behind them.

"Indeed."

He considered the matter settled and resumed the silence between them. It wasn't much further to the Double

H, and Gideon needed to think about how he was going to explain Miss Sheppard and young Andrew to his brothers. They could be as bad as Emma, when it came to his personal life. He knew Teresa would be delighted. Her husband, his foreman Mendo LaBaena, were never blessed with children, so she fussed over all the Harts as thought they were her own.

Lost in thought, Mis Sheppard's soft voice suddenly brought him back to the present.

"Mr. Hart? I assume you do go to town for church on Sundays?"

This wasn't as easy to answer as might be expected.

The preacher's words hadn't felt the same in quite some time. It was hard to feel like an honest man, when he was hiding such an awful secret.

It also didn't help that each time he did attend, he was mobbed afterward by mamas with daughters of marrying age. The ladies would fuss and coo over his daughter to showcase their "maternal instincts," ignoring the fact that Tilly hated their attentions. A dark scowl did little to scare them off, and Gideon had often been tempted to declare from the pulpit that he would sooner be six feet under than ever wed again.

His only relief was when Rhett or Ben showed up, drawing away some of the attention. And although his youngest brother, Luke, seemed to get himself in enough trouble that most mothers thought it best to limit their campaigns to the older three Harts, their daughters often felt otherwise.

"Mr. Hart?"

Miss Sheppard's gentle nudge diverted him from the irritating train of thought.

"Your family does attend ... don't they?"

"Yes, Miss Sheppard, they do. You won't have to miss a service, if that is your concern."

He watched as relief washed over her face. He felt relieved too, for a different reason. He'd managed to side-step explaining his own current relationship with the church, when she'd asked about his family and not just himself. A soft 'thank you' was her only verbal response.

He was being unkind again. Emma was probably right about Miss Sheppard and her brother being nice people, but experience had taught him about trusting too easily. Still, he found himself wanting to reassure her

"There are times when it isn't possible to get into town. Certain seasons, and weather can make it difficult. But we do have a fella named Virgil Lamb: the boys call him 'Glory.' Knows the good book better than some preachers I've met. He's one of the ranch hands, and he performs small services for those interested. It's probably not what you're used to, but it does in a pinch."

"I think that's wonderful, Mr. Hart."

"Yeah, well."

This entire ride, he'd gone from angry, to amused, to curious, then back to bothered. He'd been around Miss Sheppard for hardly an afternoon, and she already had him tied up six ways from Sunday. He didn't trust himself around her.

Gideon didn't dare say anything else.

He didn't want to start a conversation that left him with more questions than answers.

She was just a governess for his daughter, fulfilling a role that was currently needed. She was there to guide Tilly and set her on the right path. Her job was to lighten his load, not take up space in his head.

He could handle this.

Until Autumn Springs found a qualified teacher, Gideon would put up with Miss Sheppard and her little brother. He made a mental note to light a fire under the town's leaders. They needed a real teacher and a real school, so Tilly could attend it, and Miss Sheppard could go back to Portland, or anywhere that wasn't his ranch.

His eyes shifted to the gloved hand that she had clamped to the bench. He'd bet the title on the Double H that beneath that fine fabric was skin so soft and smooth, because it had never seen a day's work.

Miss Sheppard might stick around for a while, maybe even long enough for a few extra manners to fix themselves to Tilly, but it wouldn't be more than a few weeks or so before she gave up. That would be the best outcome. If Miss Sheppard left of her own volition, then he wouldn't have to face Emma's wrath, or his brothers' disapproval.

Gideon gave the reins some extra encouragement. The sooner they got to the Double H, the sooner she'd be gone.

$$4$$

Although it had only been three days since she arrived at the Double H, everyone at the ranch had made her feel right at home. Almost everyone, anyway.

Mr. Hart had pulled up to the cabin he had told her she and Andrew would share, but then seemed to change his mind at the last minute. Instead, he had Teresa settle them into the main house. Their rooms were upstairs in the large home, while Gideon and Tilly had their rooms on the main floor.

Arriving beneath the intricately carved archway of the Double H, Madeline was impressed by the large home that rose from the land. It wasn't made of stone or finely detailed masonry, like her family home in Portland, but of thick logs, likely taken from the land surrounding them. Wide stairs welcomed visitors to a porch that wrapped around the front of the home. To the right of the house was a large stump, with the handle of an axe deeply lodged like it was Montana's version of King Arthur's Excalibur. An enormous pile of firewood was stacked at the side of the house.

Inside, the central staircase wound in an open spiral to the second floor, which offered more doors and rooms than one would have expected from the outside. Her room, like Andrew's, had a simple but comfortable bed with a thick mattress covered with a colorful quilt. There was a wardrobe, chair, table and mirror, and a lovely writing desk. But it was the view from the window that took Madeline's breath away.

In the distance, mountains rose into the sky. The towering peaks appeared to defy gravity, by staying upright. At the base of the great sheets of grey rock were trees that only climbed so high before seeming to bow before the stony faces of the mountains. The panorama was unlike anything she'd experienced prior, and Madeline hoped she might still be here to witness the leaves change as fall made its appearance. She wondered if the looming mountains and their skirts of trees and foliage were the reason the town was named Autumn Springs.

Andrew was in heaven. He was surrounded by horses and all things cowboy, and once he shed his gentleman's suit for more practical attire, he practically skipped around the Double H.

After witnessing Madeline's initial attempts to alter the hand-me-down clothing for the two of them, Teresa had taken pity upon her and helped to outfit them. Madeline's fine embroidery skills had not immediately translated to alterations, but with Teresa's kind guidance, it went much faster.

Tilly was also a joy. In three short days, she had embraced combed hair, and seemed to have stopped quoting the men. Whether it was merely in Madeline's presence or truly curtailed, there was no way to know, but even if the girl was only learning to know when things were and were not appropriate, that was a start.

The children were both with her now, as they prepared for supper. The savory scent of roasting meat and vegetables wafted through the house and into her room.

"Smell's good." Andrew's healthy appetite pleased Teresa to no end, and Tilly enjoyed having another person at the table to sneak her vegetables to. Madeline kept one eye on her, but as long as she ate the majority of what she was given, there were bigger battles to fight, for now.

"I just hope there's no turnip. Yuck." Tilly stuck a finger down her throat as she looked into the mirror to meet Andrew's eyes.

"I like turnip."

"You like everything," giggled Tilly.

The two children, in spite of him being twelve, had fallen into a rhythm as though they were long lost siblings. Tilly was certainly the ringleader, but it pleased Madeline to see Andrew coming out of his shell.

Madeline quickly finished plaiting Tilly's hair before the girl became impatient.

"All done. See how lovely you look, Tilly." Madeline smiled from behind the chair and into the mirror at the girl.

Tilly tilted her head to the left and then to the right, then gently touched the hair on her head. "I think you're right. I look beautiful!" Her face lit up. "Don't I look beautiful, Andrew?"

Andrew looked up, but only shrugged and went back to looking out the window.

Madeline squeezed the girl's shoulder. "You always do."

Tilly hopped off the chair and gave Madeline a quick hug. "Can I go show Teresa? She'll want to see me, I know it."

Madeline laughed. "Of course. We will be down in a moment."

The little girl's confidence was a sure sign of a loved child, and she reminded herself to let Mr. Hart know what an admirable job he and his family were doing in raising her, if she ever had a moment alone with him.

The man was everywhere, yet nowhere at the same time.

She thought he might like to review what she had planned for Tilly, or even check in to see how things were going, but he never approached her if she didn't have the children with her. The man seemed to come inside only for coffee more than she thought any single person could drink. Any time she took the children outside, he was there, but always just far enough away that conversation would be impossible. She was tempted to holler at him to come over, exactly as she had asked Tilly *not* to. But even supposing she did, Madeline thought he was more likely to run in the opposite direction. If he really thought she was so awful, he wouldn't have allowed his daughter to be associated with her, so she wished he would speak his mind, and tell her what his concerns were.

Mr. Hart was nothing like his brothers, at least not in his dealings with her. Ben, Rhett, and Luke introduced themselves as soon as they heard of her arrival. They were open and friendly, and wonderful with Andrew, and each one as handsome as the last. Men like this would cause quite a stir if they ever entered the dining rooms and parlours in Portland. Yet, as attractive and kind as they all were, it was the somber, suspicious one that piqued her curiosity.

At dinner, gathered around the table, Madeline and Andrew took the seats that had somehow become theirs in only three days. Mr. Hart sent Bandit from the room despite Tilly's usual protest, and Madeline inwardly laughed at the man's feigned irritation with the dog. Earlier that very day, she had caught him scratching the ecstatic collie's belly—until he realized she was watching. He scowled, then quickly disappeared, leaving Bandit on his back, still looking for love.

"So, Miss Sheppard. With a few days under your belt, so to speak, what do you think of the Double H?" asked Ben.

Ben was the biggest of the Hart brothers, in breadth if not height, and while they had all been welcoming since she had arrived, Ben was certainly the sweetest. He had a twinkle in his eye that instantly removed any qualm a lady might have around a man of his size. It was interesting to see how similar the brothers looked, but how different they all were in personality.

"It might sound silly to you, but I've never seen anything like it." She closed her eyes for a moment before she spoke again. "I watched the red and orange hues of the sunset washing over the ranch last night from my window, and in that moment, I felt insignificant to the majesty of the mountains and the beauty that surrounds it."

The youngest, Luke, let out a slow whistle at the end of the table. Ben grinned.

"That's how I feel too, Miss Sheppard," he agreed.

"Though I don't think you would have worded it in such a poetic way," said Rhett, who then nodded at her. "That was the prettiest I think I ever heard it described, Miss Sheppard. I can see why Gideon hired you. If you can teach Tilly to speak like that, she might be the wife of the president one day."

"And Rhett knows all about pretty," teased Luke.

"I'd be the president, not just some wife," muttered Tilly.

"That, I'd like to see," laughed Luke.

"Watch me." Tilly whispered so softly that only Madeline could hear.

Madeline watched her young charge turn her scowl on her uncle but didn't stop her. It was enough the child didn't voice her displeasure in a loud and far less appropriate way. It was only their first week together, and Rome wasn't built in a day. Besides, Tilly shouldn't limit her dreams because she was a girl.

"I think there's no telling what Tilly will accomplish in her life, but I do know it will be something grand."

Her words were rewarded with a beaming smile from Tilly, and what could be interpreted as approval from Mr. Hart, if she was feeling optimistic.

She caught his eye, and he immediately bent back to his food, whatever she had glimpsed, gone.

"How about you, Andrew?" asked Ben. "Do you like it here? With those new duds on, you certainly look like you've been here your whole life."

Andrew gave the man a smile so big that his eyes almost disappeared. Quickly swallowing the bite of food he had in his mouth, he answered. "Best place in the whole world!"

He sounded so earnest that Madeline almost laughed out loud, until she saw all the Hart men solemnly nodding in response. It looked like Andrew had found a whole room full of people who shared his enthusiasm.

"You got that right," said Rhett. "Smart kid."

Madeline watched Andrew's cheeks flush and he sat a little higher in his chair. The Hart brothers weren't going to make it easy to convince Andrew to leave when the time came.

"And now he doesn't look like Mayor Branam? He looks like a real cowboy, doesn't he Daddy?"

Forced to look in their direction, Mr. Hart winked at Andrew, then smiled at his daughter. "Sure does, honey."

"And don't I look beautiful tonight, Daddy?"

"Yes, Tilly, you do."

"You were supposed to say it right away, Daddy. Miss Sheppard says a lady shouldn't ask for compliments, but I thought you might forget, so I'm helping you."

Mr. Hart didn't bother to hide his smile. "Thank you. It was a good reminder."

"Yeah, she says that it took a little more brushing than expected, but now that we comb it every day it's silky and smooth." A proud grin covered the little girl's face. "Now I look like Miss Sheppard, but her hair's black. She's beautiful too, right, Daddy?"

Madeline cheeks went hot, and she wished she could snap her fingers and disappear. Tilly's innocent prodding didn't seem to be making Mr. Hart any more comfortable either. He glanced over and met her eyes, he hesitated, then cleared his throat.

"Yes honey, Miss Sheppard is a beautiful lady. You both are."

Then he looked away.

There was a brief silence until Ben spoke up again. "Well, it's real nice to have you joining us, Miss Sheppard. With Emma married and living in town now ..." he paused. "Let's say the change is welcome."

Happy to find the conversation going away from her appearance, Madeline smiled at Ben.

"That's kind of you to say. I must admit that meeting your sister when I did was quite fortuitous. Without her help I certainly wouldn't be here now. And for that I am grateful."

A quiet scoff came from Mr. Hart. "She does love to help."

Ben ignored his brother and addressed Madeline. "How is Emma? She hasn't been out this way, the past few weeks, things being what they are."

"We didn't have much time together, I'm afraid, but she seemed very happy, quite ... robust."

Everyone around the table started laughing at her description. Even Andrew joined in, so as not to be left out. Perhaps she should have used another word to describe Emma's animated persona, but no other word came to mind.

"You seem to have a knack for observation, Miss Sheppard," chuckled Rhett. "Emma is indeed a whirlwind, but a storm that usually finishes with a rainbow at the end. I'm sure she would have wanted to be out here checking on you, but I have a feeling that Wes may have put his foot down on that much travel. Either way, we are all looking forward to welcoming another Hart."

"It'll be a boy," Luke stated.

"And why's that?" asked Ben.

"Lord wouldn't make Wes put up with two females like Emma," replied Luke.

"Hey!" cried Tilly.

"Luke," growled Mr. Hart. "Is that really necessary?"

Luke shrugged, unrepentant. "It ain't not necessary."

Tilly whispered to Madeline. "He needs your lessons too."

"Can't you find a way to amuse yourself without causing trouble?" Still glaring at his youngest brother, he added, "We will all be thankful for the child that comes. Boy or girl."

"I don't know," said Rhett. "Might be nice to have

another niece." He gave Tilly a wink. "This one here is pretty good."

"Thank *you*, Uncle Rhett," replied Tilly, while casting a cross look Luke's way.

Looking at her tightly squeezed lips, Madeline had a feeling that Tilly was biting her tongue to stop herself from sticking it out. Her young charge was a quick learner.

"Exactly!" agreed Ben, as he popped another chunk of beef in his mouth, which he promptly swallowed. "Having another lady around here would be good for *everyone*. Wouldn't you agree, Gideon?"

"I thought we were talking about babies." Mr. Hart gave his brother a hard look.

Ben smiled back and shrugged. "*You* are."

"Am I missing something?" asked Luke. Madeline silently wondered the same thing. There seemed to be an underlying conversation going on that she wasn't privy to.

"No," replied Mr. Hart.

At the same moment Ben said, "You usually are, little brother. But I, for one, am grateful for the pleasant company of a woman. Not all of us are afraid of the fairer—"

"I'm not afraid of their company, *big* brother. Not at all. It's their long-term ambitions I'm afraid of," interrupted Luke, smirking.

"It's okay," replied Ben. "Rhett here is too, but I think it's because he's afraid they might have a prettier face than he does."

"Whoa, there." Rhett raised his hands in mock outrage. "How am I being dragged into this? What did I do?"

Madeline wasn't sure she should be so entertained by the back-and-forth amongst the brothers, especially considering the topic, but she was fascinated just the same.

"I think that's enough," said Mr. Hart, but it didn't sound

like a suggestion. "We have two guests at our table. It would be nice if we could at least pretend to be civilized. Miss Sheppard here may be inclined to quit her position after listening to you lot."

"Well, we definitely wouldn't want that. My apologies Miss Sheppard. It appears that your lessons may need to extend beyond Tilly … and Luke." Ben's tone conveyed no remorse.

Madeline didn't bother to hide her smile. She didn't want to contradict her new employer, but she was not offended in the least.

"It's quite all right, Mr. Hart."

All four men seemed relieved.

"Miss Sheppard?" asked Tilly. "With all the Mr. Harts you're saying, how is anyone supposed to know who you're talking to."

As she answered, she gently pushed back the wisp of hair that had loosened from Tilly's plaits. "It's important to look people in the eye when speaking. It also helps to reduce any confusion."

The girl looked unconvinced.

"Tilly does make a good point," said Ben. "I was starting to get confused myself. There's far too many 'Mr. Harts' around here. If you don't mind, I'd be happy to have you call me by my given name."

"Same." Luke and Rhett spoke in unison.

"Gideon?" asked Ben. "That make sense to you?"

Mr. Hart visibly swallowed, and Madeline saw alarm in his eyes. The poor man had been backed into a corner by his brothers. He had been very clear about maintaining boundaries.

"It's all right, Mr. H—"

He cut her off before she could finish. "That'd be fine."

His words surprised her. Each time she thought he would do one thing, he did another. She didn't want to make him uncomfortable, but if they all agreed, then so should she. Mr. Hart had warned her that things were done differently here at the ranch. She would need to embrace those differences.

"I confess it will make it a little easier," said Madeline. "But only if all of you do the same."

"Excellent!" boomed Ben.

"Excellent," echoed Andrew as he grinned across the table at him.

The big man smiled back at her brother.

Madeline tried to explain the excitement her brother was feeling. "As you can tell, Andrew is also enjoying your high-spirited table. It's nice to see an entire family that shares a table for their meals. Joining you all has been a lovely change."

Gideon's head snapped up. "What do you mean?"

"Only me and Maddie eat together," offered Andrew. "I like this more."

Dropping her eyes from Gideon's searching gaze, she felt her cheek burn at the intimate information that Andrew had innocently shared.

There was a dreadful silence around the table, and Madeline wished the floor would open and swallow her whole. This family probably thought their deep connections to each other were the norm, rather than the exception. Madeline had refused to dine without Andrew in Portland, whether under her parents' or her uncle's roof. After a while she hadn't even thought it strange, it simply was. But the shocked faces around the table told her that their experiences were not shared by any of the Harts.

It was Gideon who broke the silence. "Well, Andrew, I

hope you won't mind the noise, because both you and your sister will be joining us from now on."

Lifting her gaze to Gideon, she searched his face for any sign of pity. She found none, just a determined set of his jaw. If she thought to turn him down, he was making it evident that he would not accept such an answer.

"Isn't that right, Miss—Madeline."

He made it sound like a question, but it was not. It was almost as if he were daring her to disagree. If he was, he would be disappointed.

"It is a generous offer, Gideon, thank you." Madeline gave him her most gracious smile; she could be unpredictable too.

"Oh, goody!" piped Tilly, and she placed her hand on Madeline's. "Maybe you'll stay here forever."

The new awkward silence that fell over the table at Tilly's words was quickly broken by Gideon.

"How about we let Madeline get through this week first, before we make any more plans for her." Gideon softly brushed his finger across his daughter's nose. "Sound fair?"

Tilly nodded.

"Good. Now that all that's settled, could someone pass those potatoes, before Ben and Andrew eat them all?"

Madeline noticed that he gave Andrew a reassuring smile with his jest.

Tilly leaned close to Madeline and whispered loudly. "I'm glad you're here, and don't worry about Uncle Rhett. He has nice hair, but I think yours is even prettier. Mine is too."

Madeline's hand flew up to the chignon she had twisted before she left her room. "Oh, thank you, Tilly. I think."

"It's all right," said Rhett as he looked over at his niece. "I'm inclined to agree, but we'll see if you can keep your own hair as nice as it is now." He gestured at Tilly's head. "I have a feeling a week from now, I'll be right back in second place."

Laughter erupted at the table. As good-natured conversation continued, Madeline found she was truly enjoying herself, for the first time in months.

Gideon watched Madeline from the corner of his eye, as she fell into bantering with his brothers. She'd only been at the Double H a few days, and already it felt like she'd always been here. The light-hearted talk and smiles reminded him of suppers when his parents had still been alive, and they all sat round the table sharing a meal.

She was fitting in far too easily. It didn't help with his brothers now forcing him to call Madeline by her first name. He would have looked like a heel if he'd said no, and his brothers would have been merciless. So, instead he was left with one more of his defenses down, between him and Miss Madeline Sheppard.

He was rolling her name around in his mind, deciding if it suited her or not, when he found he'd missed a question that had been thrown his way.

"Daddy? Did you hear me? Miss Madeline needs some extra things to help with my lady education."

Gideon hoped that part of that learning would be teaching Tilly not to call it that. *Lady education.* Good grief.

He addressed Madeline, "Whatever you need is fine."

She looked at him approvingly and he suddenly felt like he had just received a star on a schoolboy's test.

"Thank you. I hated to ask you so soon after arriving. I was hoping to join you on your next trip to town."

"There's a lot I need to do here, and like I said, we don't go in every day. So, it may be a few days yet."

If she was disappointed, she didn't voice it. She only gave him a quick nod. "Of course, when you can spare the time."

She was so pleasant about it that Gideon felt bad for putting her off, though he didn't know why. It wasn't that he was lying. He was busy. He was always busy. The Double H was a big operation: he couldn't just drop everything at the shopping whims of some woman. His brothers should know that too, but the questioning looks on all three of their faces indicated that he had once again, said the wrong thing.

It was Luke who fired the first shot across his bow.

"I can." Luke grinned across the table at Gideon. "I'll make the time for you, Madeline. I'm sure that there are a few stops I can make in town myself."

Why was Gideon not surprised? Luke lived for moments like these, where he could stick it to his older brothers. He narrowed his eyes on his youngest, trouble-making brother. Luke was lucky he was at the opposite end of the table. Gideon knew that Luke had no interest in Madeline, other than using her to provoke him. Luke had no interest in settling down at all. He'd sworn he'd never be shackled by marriage. Nothing like his twin, Micah, Luke preferred to sweet-talk the girls of town, but never gave away his heart. Micah had only ever loved one woman.

Gideon didn't know why he was so irritated, but he wasn't about to let Luke use Madeline as a pawn in his teasing.

"You finished in the east pasture?" asked Gideon.

"No, but Lee Manning can handle it," replied Luke.

"You'd have another man do your work for you?" It wasn't really a question.

Luke's neck flushed red at the public reprimand, and he

dropped his fork noisily on his plate. "I might ask you the same question."

Luke's insinuation was clear, and Gideon felt the heat in his cheeks. He didn't want to get into it with his hot-headed brother, certainly not in front of Tilly and the Sheppards. He took a deep breath.

"Finish the job, then you can go into town." With a thin smile he continued, "I'm sure the ladies of Autumn Springs could use a reprieve from all your attentions."

Why had he added that last part? Was it to put Luke in his place or was he hoping to stamp out any interest Madeline might have in his brother before it got started? To let her know that Luke wasn't the type to settle down. Seeing his brother's renewed grin, Gideon groaned inwardly at how easily Luke had pulled him in. Why should he even care?

Rhett opened his mouth like he was about to offer, but one look from Gideon and he snapped it shut. Good thing, because the idea of Rhett and Madeline didn't make him feel any better. Rhett was a smooth talker. What was wrong with him? He didn't want to have to be seated next to Madeline on the bumpy ride in. The rutted, uneven road meant they'd be constantly brushing up against each other. That first ride to the Double H had been difficult enough. He wasn't made of stone and he would've had to been blind not to recognize she was a beautiful woman.

But if he didn't want his brothers or one of the ranch hands taking her, there was only one option. He was about to give in to Madeline's request when Ben spoke up.

"I'd be happy to take you in, tomorrow. I have some business with Micah, and it would be nice to see Emma and Wes."

Gideon had to bite his tongue. He'd already protested too much, and he didn't want Madeline to think she was captive here at the Double H. Ben was the safest option of his brothers, but it still didn't sit right with him. Somehow Gideon felt like he was missing out on something.

"That would be lovely, Ben." She turned that bright smile on Ben, then turned back to Gideon. "If that is all right with you?"

How could he say no? Anything less than a yes would seem purposely spiteful.

"Fine. Make sure you've got a list of what you need. The next time we go in will be Sunday, and the mercantile won't be open. Andrew and Tilly can stay here and help out."

Andrew didn't say a word, but his excitement was evident.

"I will. Thank you, Gideon."

It was only the second time she'd said his given name and he found he liked the sound of it, even more than the first. Was he so starved for feminine attention? There were plenty of women in town calling his name, and not one of them made him wonder how it would sound if it were whispered in the night …

"You're coming to church again, Daddy?"

Good heavens. He needed to give his head a shake. Facing Tilly, Gideon hoped to ignore the look of surprise that was surely on Madeline's face at his daughter's question. He didn't need any extra judgement from her. The shame he placed on himself was enough.

He looked down at his sweet daughter's face. "I am, honey."

"Oh, good. Pastor Woods says you are—"

"Finish up your food." Gideon interrupted Tilly before she could repeat the preacher's opinions of what he should and should not be doing.

"I am." And she got to work clearing her plate.

Rhett generously changed the subject, knowing it was a sore spot, and Gideon spent the rest of the meal with his eyes on his plate while his thoughts ran around in his head.

He wondered what Madeline was thinking; if she thought less of him, knowing he wasn't a consistent attendee of the preacher's sermons. Then he tried to figure out why it even mattered. He'd disappointed so many people over the past several years that one more wouldn't make a difference.

When Teresa brought out dessert, Gideon's eyes happened to briefly met Madeline's. He saw no contempt there, only kindness. She looked at him no differently than she had before. Maybe she was wise enough to know that it was none of her business, and he was under no obligation to justify himself to her. Yet, her apparent lack of judgement loosened the tightness that had been forming in his chest.

Whether he liked it or not, the presence of Miss Madeline Sheppard was already causing a shift in the winds at the Double H. The only question left to be answered was, was it a cleansing breeze or the sign of an impending storm?

5

———

Even with the largest Hart brother sitting beside her in the wagon, the ride to town still wasn't as uncomfortable as it had been with Gideon. Ben kept up a running commentary on his upcoming chance to purchase the perfect horse for his stables, his younger brothers, along with the folks in town, and all their quirks. He was full of information on almost everyone, and a laughing Madeline teased him that she would mention his name as an example when people claimed that only women were prone to gossip. She didn't mind hearing it all, as it allowed her to learn so much more about Autumn Springs and its residents.

As they entered town, Madeline saw it through fresh eyes. Her last, and only, time in town had been under far different circumstances, and she was feeling much surer of herself this time around. It's funny how the need for food and shelter can cause almost everything else to fall to the wayside.

It was actually quite a bustling town. Main Street was wide enough for at least three wagons to pass through side by side. There were more people out and about than when she'd last been here, most of them men, with a smattering of women amongst them.

"My goodness," she said, inching closer to Ben. "There are far more people than when I was last here."

Ben flicked the reins and kept the horses moving forward. "Looks like payday must have hit for some of the miners. This town certainly is growing." He gave her a little nod. "Not to worry, Madeline, I expect that most of these fellas will disappear to the south end of town, once they pay off a few debts, and send telegrams back home."

"The telegraph office. Would it be possible to go there?"

"Sure. Sending something back home?"

"Yes ... well, not exactly." Madeline wasn't sure how to explain who she was sending it to, without having to provide him with details she wasn't ready to share.

Ben gave her a funny look, then shrugged. "Whatever you need. I need to see Micah. Why don't we go there first, and you can meet Nora. That's his wife. She's Emma's best friend, and definitely the angel on my sister's shoulder." He chuckled at his own joke. "Micah is Luke's twin, and while they look alike that's where it ends. Like Rhett, Micah is another studious one in our lot. And probably the reason that Luke has stayed out of real trouble as long as he has."

"Oh, no."

"Aw, I didn't really mean it like that," assured Ben. "Luke's a good guy. He's just, well, he's the youngest of all us boys, and still thinks he has something to prove."

"That's understandable. It must be hard to stand out when there are so many of you," said Madeline.

"That's for sure."

Ben's tone shared far more than he probably intended,

and Madeline wondered if the big man beside her some-times still felt small among his brothers.

"Emma mentioned Nora to me. Do you think we'll see your sister today, too?"

Ben laughed. "That's the thing about small towns, Made-line. Even if I don't know what I'm doing, guaranteed someone else does." He nodded toward the folks along the boardwalk. "Rumors travel fast around here. She's probably already heard we're here. I'd be surprised if we didn't see her before long."

As they made their way to the doctor's office, Madeline noticed both covert and outright stares in her direction. Did they know her circumstances? Were they judging her for being unmarried and taking a position out at the Double H? Or was it simple curiosity?

They'd almost arrived at Micah's when a familiar voice rang out.

"Madeline! Ben!" Emma was waving at them from the boardwalk, a blonde woman with an air of sweetness at her side. "We heard you were in town."

"Told ya," whispered Ben, as he brought the wagon to a halt next to the ladies.

Ben jumped down and helped Madeline down before he went and greeted the ladies. He looked down at his sister, in mock horror. "Should you even be walking around at this point?"

Emma laughed and swatted at his arm. "Don't you dare let Wes hear you say that." She turned to squeeze Madeline's hands. "Madeline. I want you to meet my dearest friend in the world. Nora Hart."

"Hello, Nora. It's a pleasure to meet you," said Madeline.

"This is wonderful. I've been listening to Emma despair over the past several days that you wouldn't be back in town, and she couldn't go out with me to the Double H, that it's almost a relief to meet you in person."

"How unfair, Nora. You paint a terrible picture of me." She paused. "But also, accurate. How are you doing at the Double H? How is it working out with Gideon?"

Nora cleared her throat.

"Gideon's daughter," smiled Emma. "You know what I meant."

"That's my cue to leave," said Ben. "Ladies, I trust I can leave Madeline in your capable hands? She has a few things to pick up, but we won't be here all day. Why don't we meet back at your place Nora? Once you're all done."

"Perfect!" cried Emma, as she joined her elbow to Madeline's.

Madeline watched as Nora and Ben exchanged a knowing look, like this was something they were quite used to.

"We'll be back, Ben. Micah is in the office. He's just finishing up with a patient. Nothing serious, so he won't be long," said Nora.

Ben touched the brim of his hat, and quickly left.

"So?"

Emma's excitement once again reminded Madeline of Miss Austen's Emma. It would have been slightly more endearing if it wasn't so misguided.

"It's going very well. At least I think so. Tilly is such a lovely girl, and she's eager to learn. Andrew has never been so happy."

"That's wonderful, Madeline," said Nora.

"Yes, it is," agreed Emma. "And how is Gideon? Is he … happy, too?"

Madeline almost laughed at Emma's less than subtle question. "I believe your brother is content with the arrangement. We haven't really spoken much; he seems quite busy most of the time."

"There's lots of men to work," muttered Emma. Then she continued, "I was hoping he might take more of an interest in things."

This time Madeline let her laugh slip out. "If you think that your brother has an interest in anything other than his ranch and his daughter, I'm afraid I will disappoint you."

"Was she that obvious?" smiled Nora, innocently. Then she turned to her friend. "You really are."

"I have no expectations! I simply thought this practical arrangement might have some romantic potential. Forgive me," sighed Emma.

"I promise you; your brother has no such thoughts. Certainly not regarding me. He seems like a good man, but I'm afraid your match-making efforts are for naught."

"I know he can be a grump, but don't you at least think he's attractive?"

"Of course, but—"

"See!" clapped Emma. "You think he's a good man, and you think he's handsome, that's a wonderful start."

"That's where it ends," added Madeline firmly. "To be fair, Gideon is probably still grieving his wife. The last thing he wants is a woman living in his home with thoughts of romance in her head."

"Thoughts of romance? A first name basis?" Emma seemed undeterred. "Cordelia has been gone for quite some time. Not to be cruel, but Tilly was just a babe. Perhaps if Gideon knew you were interested ..."

Madeline was starting to see the similarity between Emma and Luke. "If he knew I was interested, not that I am, I would be out of a job. A job I desperately need, mind you."

Nora placed a hand on Emma's back. "Fair enough. Why

don't we get the items you need from the stores and then retreat from the heat with some cold tea. Then you can meet Micah."

Madeline shot Nora a grateful smile. "Thank you, that sounds lovely." She placed her hand on Emma's arm that was still intertwined with hers. "And thank you. Your kindness to Andrew and I was a lifesaver."

Appearing mollified, Emma returned the smile. "All right. Let's stop by Garvin's Mercantile. They will have most of what you might need, and I know Mrs. Garvin is looking forward to meeting you."

The trio made their way to Garvin's Mercantile, where she met the friendly Mrs. Garvin and saw the wide selection of items the store carried. It was more than she expected, but then again, so was everything she had experienced so far in Autumn Springs. Everyone gave their opinions as to what Madeline needed to pick up for herself as well as for Andrew and Tilly. She ended up leaving with a few more things than she expected.

They waited for her outside the telegraph office as she sent her note to her father's barrister in Portland, explaining what happened and where she was now. Neither woman asked any further details, but Madeline thought Emma might have filled Nora in on what she knew.

Promising to visit again on Sunday, the ladies walked her back to Ben, where she had the chance to meet the town's doctor, and Nora's husband, Micah Hart. He was a quiet contrast to his boisterous twin Luke, and it was obvious that Nora and Micah were a perfect match. They seemed so content in each other's presence. A tiny twinge of envy went through her as she watched the loving couple, but she was happy for Nora to have found such a true love.

They didn't stay long afterward. Ben's business was

finished, and Madeline didn't want to be away too long from the Double H. It had taken some convincing for her to leave Andrew behind and she wanted to return as soon as possible. Madeline also wanted Gideon to know she wasn't shirking her duties to his daughter.

Their return to the ranch seemed to go quickly. Madeline was caught up in telling Ben the things she was excited to be sharing with Tilly in their lessons as they approached the Double H.

In the distance, she could see a number of the men sitting on or leaning against one of the big corrals. The men were cheering, Gideon among them. At first, she couldn't see what was happening in the corral, but as they drew closer, Madeline realized it was Andrew, and he was on a horse.

Then he wasn't. He must have fallen, since he disappeared from sight.

She gasped, covering her mouth with her hand, and tried to stand up in the moving wagon. Ben steadied her and brought the wagon round in the direction of the corral.

Her heart was racing. "What are they doing to him? I knew I should have brought him with me." Fear for her brother's safety surged through her, mingling with guilt for having left him behind.

"I'm sure he's fine. He's just learning. From the looks of it, he's doing pretty good." Ben's voice was calm, and he didn't seem worried at all.

Madeline let out a sigh of relief when Andrew came back into sight, atop the giant horse. The beast looked so much bigger with her brother in the saddle.

"He's never been on a horse before," explained Madeline. "Can you not drive faster?"

She knew her tone was sharp. It wasn't Ben's fault. The

sooner they got there, the sooner she could remove her brother from danger and give Gideon Hart a piece of her mind.

Ben remained quiet and clicked at the horses to go faster.

This time when the wagon stopped, Madeline didn't wait for someone to help her down. Anger propelled her from her seat. She was marching over to Gideon, as Ben called out that he would take the packages into the house for her. Madeline waved her thanks without turning and kept right on marching.

Seeing her come, the ranch hands stepped back from the rails, leaving Gideon alone.

"Mr. Hart!"

The man must have heard her coming, yet he hadn't turned around. While she waited with hands on hips, he only took off his hat, ran his fingers through his thick hair, and then put it back down on his head.

He still hadn't turned around when he spoke. "I thought the plan was to be on a first name basis around here ... Miss Sheppard."

His response brought her to a fresh new level of anger.

"I can't believe it."

Gideon nodded. "I can't believe it either."

"You're mocking me. You think I'm wrong?"

"I won't think anything until you tell me what it is that you are angry about."

The man was toying with her, and every moment he continued, her brother could be in danger.

"How dare you! If you won't stop this, then I will."

Starting to duck under the fence, she was pulled back by a strong hand on her elbow.

"He's fine. Don't run in there and embarrass the poor kid."

Madeline looked down at Gideon's hand which still held her arm, then snapped her eyes back to meet his. "Let me go."

"No." It was said so casually that it took her a moment to respond.

"No? I beg your pardon. Who do you think you are? He could be hurt!"

"He's not."

"He's just a child," hissed Madeline.

"But he's not a baby. You need to quit treating him like one."

"You know nothing about us."

"I'm very aware of that," replied Gideon. "But he's doing fine. Everyone falls. His arms will get stronger over time."

"What do you know? This is a working ranch with working men. He's not built like them. How can you not see the difference? It's not so easy for him." Madeline jerked her arm, still in his grasp. "Are you going to let me go?"

"Are you still going in there?" He sighed and let go of her. "Just look at him first and tell me what you see."

Madeline took her eyes from Gideon to watch Andrew.

Sweaty hair was plastered to his head, but he was smiling. He was happy, and he wasn't hurt, certainly not in any dangerous way. The men around the corral were shouting encouragement, not laughing, and one of the young hands was nearby, ready to jump in if there was any real danger.

The tension left her shoulders as her anger dwindled, and she was left with an annoyed embarrassment. To be fair, she wasn't sure if she was annoyed more by Gideon, or herself.

"I'm his sister," she defended. "We only have each other." A traitorous tear rolled down her face. She hated crying in front of people and doing it with Gideon next to her was even worse.

Gideon's face softened, and he gently used his thumb to wipe the tear away as he looked down at her. "I understand that, more than you know. Hear me when I say I would never allow Andrew to be hurt. Never. But you need to loosen the reins a little. You're acting more like a mother hen, than a sister."

The tenderness of his touch and gentle tone removed the last dregs of her irritation. Once again, Gideon had surprised her. In that brief moment she could understand why the women of Autumn Springs could be attracted to the man.

She hated to admit it, but he was right. Over time, she had become a fretting mother, when she needed to be an encouraging sister. Their age difference lent itself to the fact, but there was more to it than that.

She was jealous.

In town, she had seen the love between Nora and Micah, and the way that both Emma and Mrs. Garvin spoke affectionately of their husbands. Even if her parents hadn't died, a true love match hadn't been in her future. True love was for books and plays, not reality. Yet here, in Autumn Springs, it seemed that fantasy was more the norm instead of the exception. Her life had never been like that, and it never would be. She'd come to terms with knowing that the only real love she might have was the innocent adoration of her brother. They would always have each other.

At least, that was what she had thought. But from the moment Andrew had seen his first Hart, he began to pull away from her. She couldn't blame him. They had all accepted him without question, and who wouldn't want that? He was fitting in more than she ever could.

Was that why she had reacted so harshly to the situation and to Gideon? Did she feel like she was being replaced by him, in her brother's heart? It was a foolish thought, barely worthy of thinking, but she had lost so much, so quickly. It was hard not to feel worried.

"You could be right," she admitted.

Turning her attention back to Andrew, her teeth gnawed at her lower lip as she watched him wobble and fall, then get back up again. He could have used a rail to get on: nobody would have said a word. But Andrew wanted to get on a horse like the other men, even though he was half their size. He wasn't crying and he wasn't complaining, but he repeated the process so often that she nearly cried out for him to stop as she gripped the rail.

Gideon placed his hand over top hers, his touch warm and reassuring, then he pulled it back to the rail in front of him.

"I know it's hard on the heart, but you'll see, it will all be worthwhile," his words were soft and kind, and it amazed Madeline, how many sides there were to this man. It gave her hope that they could be friends, that the distance between them was not as far as she had thought.

"Thank you, Gideon. I'm sorry for—"

"It's fine," Gideon broke in. "He's your brother. He's lucky to have you looking out for him."

"In that case, I would be remiss if I didn't say that horse does look a little big for him," ventured Madeline. "You didn't want to try a pony first?"

Gideon let out a low laugh, a sound that rumbled from his chest and settled itself in hers. It was like a sound that was still testing itself out after a long hibernation. She wondered why he held it back. Maybe it was only with her that he did.

"I didn't want to insult him by using Tilly's little pony. But you're probably right; I'll look to remedy that. Will that make you feel better about the whole thing? I hope so, because that is one boy who won't be dissuaded. He's got cowboying on the brain, and I don't think that's going to change anytime soon."

Watching as the huge horse continued to pull at the reins, she silently prayed it would give up its protest to her brother's attempts and settle down. Maybe it was better if she didn't stay to watch.

"All right," she conceded. "You will both insist on doing as you please, anyway. But let me give you one warning."

"Oh? What's that?" said Gideon, as he gave her a half-smile.

"If I start hearing anyone around here start calling him 'Shooter', or 'Dead-Eye' that will be the end of everything."

"Really?" Gideon raised one brow at her, then continued before she could respond. "Well, seeing as we haven't started any shooting lessons, *yet*; I think you're safe."

Madeline couldn't believe her ears. Gideon had a straight face as he spoke, so she couldn't tell if he was joking or not.

"I hope I am making myself clear, sir, when I say that you may put him on a horse, but don't you dare put a gun in his hands."

"It hadn't really crossed my mind, but now that you mention it ..."

"You wouldn't dare?" gasped Madeline.

"Wouldn't I?"

She stiffened. He couldn't be serious.

"If you even think about it, I will ... I will ..."

"What, exactly, will you do, Madeline?" He leaned in so close she could feel the heat of his body.

Her head only reached his shoulder, but she narrowed her eyes on him and boldly held his gaze. Amusement flickered across his normally stoic face, and she realized he was playing with her. The man was as incorrigible as he was confusing.

"You're teasing me."

"I am," he admitted. "I apologize." He looked anything but sorry, and grinned.

Heavens. When the man decided to truly smile, it changed everything.

"You're as bad as your brothers."

"Must be in our blood," winked Gideon.

Madeline wondered if this is what he might have been like before he lost his love. Before he was left with a broken heart, and a little girl to care for.

Now, more than ever, she knew she needed to help him. Not because he'd asked her to, but because he deserved the help. He had been through so much, and if there was one thing she understood, was how the heavy weight of responsibility and loss could change one's life.

She looked back to Andrew. He was continuing to try and was getting closer to swinging himself up into the saddle. Madeline could only imagine how sore and tired his arms must be.

"He keeps going," she didn't bother to hide the admiration in her voice.

"He isn't the only one learning something today. He's giving every man here a lesson in grit."

"Thank you for not letting me take that away from him, Gideon," said Madeline. "I would hate to have taken this chance from him."

Gideon nodded.

"I'll leave you boys to your *fun*." She moved away from him, then turned back. "Where's Tilly?"

"Probably trying to sneak something from the kitchen. She and that dog of hers have a nose for freshly baked treats." Gideon gazed past her to the main house, and he smiled. "Her ears must have been burning."

Tilly was exiting the back of the house, each hand holding a treat high up, as Bandit capered around trying to steal them.

Madeline laughed. "You were right."

He shook his head at the sight of his daughter and her dog. "You give lessons on dog manners?"

"No, I do not," replied Madeline. "But I can see they're needed. Any advice?"

"Nope, I'm sticking with horses and cattle. Good luck."

Gideon turned his back to her and shouted encouragement at Andrew, signalling he was done talking. Madeline wasn't offended. Their conversation had been far more than she had expected. She was also excited to show Tilly what she had picked up at the Garvin's Mercantile.

Meeting the girl and her pup halfway, she re-directed them back to the house.

GIDEON LET OUT a deep breath as he turned his back on Madeline. That had been the most fun, and the most uncomfortable, conversation he could ever recall. He never should have touched her but seeing that tear on her cheek had him wishing he could wipe all her hurt away. She made him feel like he wanted to protect her, that he needed to.

Those big blue eyes looking up at him, so nervous.

Maybe he should have asked her first but teaching Andrew how to saddle and mount a horse had not been his in his plans for the day.

He'd been talking with Booker when he noticed Andrew loitering about nearby. Whether it was in the barns or at the corral, Andrew was there. Seeing the boy wasn't leaving any time soon, Gideon had called out to him.

"Aren't you and Tilly supposed to be helping Teresa, this morning?"

The boy scampered towards him, pleased he was being acknowledged. "Yes, sir."

"Then why aren't you there?" asked Gideon.

"Teresa said find you. *Stop talking my ears off about horses*," Andrew mimicked Teresa, then he gave Gideon a big smile. "Now I'm here."

It was hard to ignore the tickle of a smile at his own lips. There was something endearing about Andrew. His smile made a fella want to match it with his own.

"I can see that."

"Yeah," nodded Andrew, then he squinted up at Gideon. "You said you'd teach me to ride."

"When I have time, but I don't know when that will be."

"Okay." There was no disappointment on his upturned face. He seemed to be thinking really hard, then he spoke. "I will be real close. I don't want miss when you are ready."

Gideon looked heavenward. Andrew wasn't sassing him; he sincerely meant every word. How on earth could a man say no to that?

"Fine, but don't go peppering me with a bunch of questions like you did Teresa. I'm busy and there's lots to do."

He had to make sure that Andrew knew that they weren't going to be best friends. In time Madeline would be moving on, and that meant the kid would too, no point in getting too attached. Either one of them.

"Yes, sir. I can be real quiet."

"Good."

"Maddie said stay away, cuz you can be ..." He hesitated and closed his eyes, like he was trying to find the word Madeline had used. "Bothered."

Oh, she did, did she?

Gideon pulled off his hat and drew the back of his hand across the heat on his forehead, before putting it back on with a sigh. Andrew quickly did the same thing with the hat he must have gotten from one of the men. It was real hard not to like the kid.

"Your sister sure has a lot to say," said Gideon.

"Yeah," replied Andrew.

Gideon started walking and his little shadow followed. True to his word, Andrew remained silent. Smiling, nodding or waving each time Gideon looked his way. Kid was like a puppy following him everywhere. He was starting to feel a little sympathy for Early, their father's friend and long-time ranch hand, who'd spent years with two generations of Harts trailing along behind him.

He was finishing up in the tack shed, when Andrew, sitting on an old wooden bench, pulled an apple out of his pocket. He shined it on his shirt before biting into it. He noisily munched away, until Gideon turned and looked at him with a scowl. Then Andrew pressed his lips together and he snacked on the treat only a little more quietly.

There was no point in putting it off. Gideon wasn't getting much done anyway. He might as well get Andrew on a horse before his sister got back. Then, Andrew could show her what he'd learned while she was off in town.

Pointing to Andrew's apple, Gideon said, "You got another one of those?"

He could see very well the strained outline of another apple in the boy's pocket. He must be taking lessons from Ben on stockpiling food.

Eyes lighting up, Andrew pulled out the barely hidden apple, rubbed it vigorously across his chest and held it out to Gideon, then patted the empty space on the bench beside him.

He tried to ignore the tug in his chest, but it was harder to do than he expected. He took the apple and accepted the seat. Once they were finished, Gideon took Andrew out to the corral.

And now he was watching Andrew steadying in the saddle, and catching a glimpse of Madeline walking away, his daughter's hand in hers. It was like the world was telling him the one thing he didn't want to hear, so he kept his attention on Andrew.

It had come as a surprise, but the kid had plenty of determination. His whole body would be aching tomorrow. Andrew probably hadn't been sent out to chop wood anytime he stepped out of line, like the Hart boys. Though even if he had, Gideon had a feeling the boy was probably better behaved.

Andrew spent more time with his backside in the dirt than the saddle, but he didn't quit. He was already working harder than some of the men that had drifted through the Double H over the years. He might not have much size, but he had the heart of a cowboy, and that was worth far more.

Andrew ... the kid needed a cowboy's moniker if they were going to rub the city off him. With Madeline putting her foot down on nicknames like 'Shooter', Gideon figured he better be careful with what he chose. He didn't think she'd like 'Ace' or 'Bulldog' any more than the others. She was right, none of those would have suited him. He was still a boy, not some grizzled old cow punch.

Andy. Andy was perfect. It fit him like a glove.

Gideon hollered at him. "Looking good out there, Andy! Keep it up!"

If Gideon had bet Andy's smile couldn't have gotten any bigger, he'd have lost that wager. An enormous grin covered the boy's face from ear to ear. Managing this time to stay on the horse, Andy yelled back to Gideon. "Andy!"

He nodded back; he could feel Andy's happiness from here. It was funny, how filling another's cup could feel so good.

"Andy?" Ben joined him at the rails of the corral. "Suits him."

"It does." Gideon glanced briefly at his brother, then went back to watching the boy as Billy guided him around the corral.

"Billy looks as pleased as Andy out there," said Ben.

Gideon gave a short laugh. "McCarty's just happy he's not the youngest fella out here anymore."

Ben let out a chuckle at the likely assessment.

"Get what you needed in town?" asked Gideon.

"I did, and I know you're thinking it, so I'll just tell you now: I was nowhere near Belle's Palace."

Gideon hadn't been thinking that at all. He knew that was behind Ben now. At least he hoped it was. His brother hadn't touched any cards in almost two years. And despite Floyd Keller's taunting, there was no point in living in the past.

Glad he hadn't said that last part out loud, Gideon mentally laughed at his own hypocrisy.

"I wasn't thinking that. Madeline get everything she needed?"

"I'm guessing everything and more. We met Emma and Nora," Ben told him, chuckling. He said it like that explained everything. It did.

"Good," replied Gideon.

"You work it out between the two of you?" asked Ben.

Gideon frowned. "What do you mean?"

"The way she hauled out from that wagon, I wasn't sure you'd be joining us for supper," Ben laughed.

"Ah, yeah, it's fine." He pressed his lips together before he answered. "She came in hot, but she cooled down fairly quick."

Ben laughed. "You're lucky."

They watched Andy for a while. Gideon had a feeling the kid was going to sleep well tonight.

"You know, I think it's good having Madeline here. And she sure likes Tilly. Not that it's hard to do. She couldn't stop talking about her," said Ben.

That caught his attention. "Oh, yeah?"

"She thinks Tilly's a sweetheart. Smart too, and that you've done a good job with her, considering."

"Considering? What is that supposed to mean?" Was Madeline surprised that a man like him could raise a good kid?

"Nothing. She was asking about Cordelia and felt bad for you. Probably from Emma."

"She was asking about me and Cordelia?" Gideon felt his grip on the rail tighten.

Ben took a step back. "That's not what I said. The only thing she asked about was if Tilly got that golden mop from her mother. That's all."

"Why?"

"I expect she was curious. You can't blame her, Tilly's the only straw-haired one out of all of us," explained Ben.

"What's hair got to do with anything?"

Ben held up a hand. "Nothing, it was only an observation." He shook his head. "Geez."

Gideon realized his overreaction wasn't helping anything. Madeline couldn't suspect anything. How could she? It was only natural to be curious about the mother of the girl in her charge. She was probably only making conversation.

"You all right?" asked Ben.

"Yeah, I'm fine."

"Man, if I knew that me leaving your side for a few hours would make you so grumpy, I never would have left," teased Ben. He was keeping it light, like he always did, so Gideon laughed even though he wasn't feeling it.

This is what Cordelia had done to him. Left him constantly suspicious and assuming the worst.

He smiled at his brother, to reassure him that he was fine, but the gesture didn't reach his eyes. He just had to keep smiling, and silently curse the day he had ever married Cordelia.

6

<hr>

Sitting in his office after an early breakfast, Gideon found his eyes drawn to the window that faced his old place. It had been at least a year since he had stepped foot in that cabin. He hated going in there. It was a reminder of all the mistakes he'd made.

His plan had been to have Madeline and Andrew situated out there, but when it came time to drop them off, he couldn't do it. Having them in the house was probably more convenient anyway, but it was a whole lot harder to avoid her. He could hear her talking to Andrew in the house now, probably discussing their plans for the day.

Young Andrew was another thing. It was impossible not to like the kid. His interest in the ranch and everything about it allowed Gideon to see the Double H through fresh eyes. Sometimes, when you see the same thing every day, you forget how amazing it can be. Gideon had always loved horses as a boy, but over the years, the business side of the ranch took more of him, and he stopped taking the time to enjoy the things he loved. Spending time with Madeline's brother was a good reminder for him to slow down a little.

He laughed quietly as he recalled Madeline storming over to him when she and Ben got back from town. From the corner of his eye, he'd watched her leap from the wagon like she was part hound, and it had taken everything he had not to start laughing. As a woman who normally exuded gentility, there was something appealing about this impassioned side of her.

He was also impressed that, as quickly as her ire rose, it dissipated in the face of truth. That was an unusual trait, in either man or woman. Miss Madeline Sheppard was turning out to be far more difficult to ignore than he'd first hoped. And if his plan was to avoid her, he was doing a poor job of it.

Problem was, he didn't want to.

Blast Emma. Gideon hated when she was right.

His sister was probably regaling her poor husband with her triumph over her brooding brother. Wes was a saint to put up with her, especially these last few months. Married, and being in the family way, had Emma thinking that everyone else wanted the same.

For years he'd done a fine job of sidestepping every woman who was pushed in his path. He'd made it clear that no amount of good intent or meddling machinations were going to get him anywhere near an altar ever again. He had Tilly and that was all his heart needed. He didn't need to be burned twice, and neither did his daughter. It wasn't just him he was protecting, it was Tilly too.

But now here he was, enjoying each interaction he had with Madeline, and it was hard not to notice how she already cared for Tilly, and the respect she'd already garnered from his brothers. Even Luke placed her in a different category than he did the other ladies in town. He was teasing her like a sister, not a woman.

Gideon wanted to believe that Madeline Sheppard might be different, but if wishes were horses, beggars would ride. Gideon couldn't afford to be wrong, but as much as he tried to sweep thoughts of the raven-haired woman from his mind, her image lingered.

Hoping to shake whatever had taken hold of him, he set out to the yard and began chopping wood. The distraction didn't help, it just added to the stacks along the house, so Gideon headed to the barn and saddled up his horse.

Gideon spent the rest of the morning riding fence. He soon found himself near the site of Cordelia's accident. There was no sign now of where the buggy had overturned, but the image was burned in his mind as if it had only been a day, not years ago. Early was the only one who knew what really happened that day, and he'd promised to take it to his grave. How it even came to be such a mess, Gideon still didn't understand.

Hoping to escape the direction of his thoughts, he turned away from the memory and set off at a gallop.

He reined in his mount to let the beast rest, and sat still as the steam from the horse's effort formed in the morning air. He felt like he was always running; trying to stay one step ahead of the truth. And now he was running from the temptation of Miss Madeline Sheppard.

Gideon knew he was being foolish, but everything had happened so quickly, he needed more time to figure out how he was going to handle the woman and her presence on the Double H. Andy wasn't the problem, it was like the boy had always been here. But that set of blue eyes sure was. He didn't know her story, and she wasn't exactly forthcoming. Emma had referred to a 'situation', but Gideon didn't know any more than that.

He'd agreed to Emma's idea because his daughter

needed to quit spitting and quoting rough men. He'd had no intention of making it more complicated than that. He thought he'd set his mind to it. But every time he saw Madeline, every time he talked to her, his resolve waned. She was like a walking reminder of all the mistakes he'd made in the past, and yet here he was, thinking he'd like to make them again. Made a man think he was half crazy.

Kicking his mount into motion, Gideon was still a good few miles from home when he saw Early appear in the distance. He shouldn't have been surprised.

Sighing, he watched as the old cowpoke, who'd been on the Double H since a lariat was their only corral, rode closer. One of the first men to join them at the Double H, Early had shared a deep friendship with his father. When Logan Hart died, Early had done his best to take on the some of the role. He usually shared his wisdom through stories, although when he was riled up, Early got real direct.

Gideon wondered which version was riding up on him now.

"Early," he acknowledged.

"Thought I might find you out here," replied the old man.

"You have." Gideon wasn't saying anything until he knew what Early was about.

"Boys rode this line last week. You making sure they did it right?" asked Early.

Gideon didn't know what Early was getting at yet, but he was sure it wasn't about fences. "You got something to say, just say it."

Early's eyes narrowed at his tone, but all he said was, "Miss Sheppard seems to be a fine addition to the Double H."

"Yeah. Tilly seems to like her."

"And you?"

"She's doing a good job, I guess. Seems to be fitting in."

"That all then?"

They stared at each other for a moment, then Gideon slid off his horse and leaned against the nearby fence. He bent to pluck a long blade of grass by his boot and rolled it between his fingers.

Joining him, Early folded his arms on the top rail and looked out silently to the field beyond Gideon's back.

"I don't know what I'm doing anymore, Early."

"Most of us don't."

He gave a snort to Early's response. "Yeah, well, it's not like I'm Luke, or even Ben and Rhett. I have a lot of people counting on me to keep this ranch running and a little girl that I need to do right by."

"Seems hiring Miss Sheppard fits with that."

Gideon didn't respond. Having help with Tilly was a good thing, but somehow it felt like a failure on his part.

"I was doing okay, wasn't I?"

He felt Early look at him but didn't turn to meet his gaze.

"You were. You are. But that's not what this is about. You remember those first years out here. The old house?"

"I remember," replied Gideon.

"You recollect how many calves we fit in that front entryway during calving season, that one awful winter? Wasn't sure those poor critters were going to make it. Near froze to death."

Gideon chuckled at the memory. "Six of 'em. Mama was fit to be tied when they warmed up enough to get curious in the middle of the night, and make their way into the rest of the house. She wasn't expecting that. None of us were. That rug of hers was never the same."

"Don't expect she thought she'd be washing bovines

'stead of her boys in that new tub your daddy bought for her, neither." Early let out an amused snort. "She was a good woman, your mama."

Gideon cleared his throat. "That she was."

"Point is, she was willing to try something different, because what they'd been doing wasn't working. Couldn't leave 'em out in the pasture. The Double H had one of the few herds that survived that long winter. Gave your parents a real jump on the other ranches. Helped to build what you have now: something pretty special, if you ask me. Your mama wasn't too proud to do what had to be done. Your folks chose a little discomfort and a bit of a mess to create a future for themselves."

"This is more than a little discomfort, Early."

"Is it? Or is that just what you're telling yourself?"

Gideon let the question hang between them for a few minutes before he answered.

"I don't know what's come over me. I thought I had a handle on this. I thought, truth is, I don't know what I'm thinking anymore, Early. Miss Sheppard is ... is a beautiful woman," said Gideon.

"She is."

"But there's plenty of pretty women in Autumn Springs."

"There are."

"So, this one shouldn't be any different, and she's working for me. Besides, I don't know hardly anything about her. You'd think I'd have learned my lesson. That I would know better than to be taken in by a pretty face."

"That all you think she is?"

"No. Course not. She's good with Tilly, she's intelligent, she's committed to her family." Gideon sighed, then added. "And has a smile that can light up the room."

Early gave a soft chuckle. "Doesn't sound so bad."

"No. No, it doesn't. Yet here I am, wondering what to do. You got any answers, old man?"

"Oh, these old bones got some ideas, but you aren't ready to hear it. Not yet."

"Try me," said Gideon.

"All right." Early waited only a moment, before he laid it out "You ever think it's time to stop living in the past?"

Gideon's lips clenched together. Maybe he didn't want to hear where this was going, after all. "I'm trying not to repeat it, Early."

"None of that was your fault. You couldn't control what happened. I don't blame you for it, and neither would your family, if they knew." He quickly added, "don't worry, your secret's safe with me. But it's time you moved on."

"You don't know what it's like."

Early shook his head, scoffing. "I do know what it's like to lose the only woman I've ever loved. It's a pain you've got no idea about."

"I—"

"No. You don't. Truth is, I think you feel bad because you never really even liked Cordelia. You made a bad decision. Maybe it's time for you to be honest with yourself, even if you're still lying to everyone else. One bad thing happening doesn't make the whole world bad. You can't paint every woman with the same brush, Gideon. Only fools and children reason that way."

"You're calling me a fool?" Gideon frowned, but Early ignored him and kept on talking.

"Least you got Tilly out of that whole mess. That child is a light, in what can be a dark world." Early's voice cracked. "You know what I'd give, to see my wife Rosalee again? To see my sweet little Grace, to hold her in my arms, and hear that giggle once more?"

Gideon felt sick thinking of all Early had lost. The man's words struck a chord of truth, one he hadn't wanted to admit.

"I'm sorry, Early."

"Sorry don't do me any good, or you neither. Be thankful for what you got. Right now, that's a chance for your little girl to have even more folks to love her. Worrying about anything else is a waste of time. If there is a plan laid out for you, you aren't going to stop it."

"I'm just trying to raise my daughter. Nothing else," said Gideon.

"I know," replied Early. He turned so his back was to the fence and gazed in the direction of the Double H with Gideon. "You know what your mama used to say, the years the crops were bad?"

"No," said Gideon.

"With you five strapping boys and that spirited sister of yours, she'd say the only thing they were raising was a ruckus."

"She must have wondered what her and Pa had been thinking, having such a passel of kids. Do you think she ever had second thoughts?"

Early shook his head. "Oh, no. Your mama loved every minute of it. She knew that even when it feels like the earth is shaking, at least you know you're still living. It won't always be easy, but you got to start living again."

The old man was driving his point home, but Gideon wasn't sure it was the same. His parents hadn't had to worry about the kind of secret he held, the one even Early didn't know, that he had vowed would never see the light of day.

This little talk needed to end. The whole situation was exhausting, and Gideon still had work to do. Hoping Early would understand, he changed the direction of the conversation.

"I hope you're giving my brothers the same sage advice about life. Luke could use a little reining in."

Early chuckled. "That one's still trying to figure himself out. He'll be okay, he just needs time."

Gideon shook his head. "Can you tell him to hurry it up? Anything I tell him, he's likely to do the opposite."

"Your mama knew about that too." Early, kicked his heel into the dirt, then grinned at him. "She'd say, you can always tell a Hart, but you can't tell 'em much. She wasn't wrong."

"No," said Gideon. "No, she wasn't."

7

———

"What's this?"

Tilly rubbed her finger along the intricate woodwork on the chest pushed against the wall of the parlour. She was trying to avoid picking up the embroidery needle again, and apparently a discussion on furniture was preferable to needlework. Madeline hid her smile; she didn't want to let the little girl know how much she agreed.

"You've never seen it before?"

"I don't know." Tilly bit her lip. "I don't think so."

It was odd for the piece to be here in the parlour. That spot would have been perfect for a piano. But this wasn't Portland, and perhaps it held a memory that the Harts wished to be reminded of, rather than tucked away. Madeline assumed the chest had belonged to Tilly's mother, or possibly Gideon's mother; she was surprised that as inquisitive and curious as the little girl was, she had never peeked inside.

"It's a hope chest."

"What's that?" Tilly sat down, away from her attempts

with the needle. She looked like she was hoping for a very long story.

Madeline gave her a brief description, then pointed to the fabric waiting on the table. She was on to Tilly's tricks to avoid tasks she wasn't interested in.

"So, it's just filled with stuff for when you get married?"

"That's part of it, yes." Madeline watched as Tilly's mind processed the new information. It was always interesting to see how the little girl interpreted the world around her.

"Why call it 'hope'? Just call it 'marriage' chest."

"Marriage?"

"Yeah," replied Tilly.

"Yes," corrected Madeline. "I think it is because it holds the hopes and dreams of a young lady."

"You said towels and dishes. Why are they hoping for that boring stuff? Who dreams about plates?" Tilting her head, she waited for an answer.

"They don't, not really. More for a good match and a good life."

Tilly stuck out her tongue as if the whole idea was distasteful, then wrinkled her nose. "I don't think I want one of those."

"You may one day."

"Do you?"

This was not a conversation she wanted to have with a little girl. And how was she supposed to respond, when she didn't even have an answer?

"I trust that the path I take is the one I'm meant to be on."

Tilly scratched at the back of her neck. "I don't know about that, but I don't need a good husband, ever. Lee Manning says all you need is a good horse and full belly." She shrugged. "That sounds a whole lot better to me."

Swallowing her laugh, she nodded and dipped her head, hoping Tilly wouldn't see her grin. Tilly had an innocent way of breaking down the world, and often her observations were right on the nose. Perhaps Madeline should pay a little more attention to all the cowboy wisdom, so readily available at the Double H.

"I think anything sounds better to you than picking up that needle again, young lady. See if you can do a few more stitches. I can already see an improvement."

Dragging her feet across the floor, Tilly went back to the table. Picking up the fabric, she let out an exaggerated sigh. Madeline checked on Andrew as he sat on the long reading bench built in below the window. He was looking longingly at the barns in the distance.

"Why do I have to do this? I want to be a cowboy."

"Cowboys don't just ride horses, Andrew. There's a lot more they are required to do."

Ignoring the muttered reminder of *Andy* from her brother, she tapped the book he'd pushed away. "I thought you would like this story. It's all about horses. I was so excited when I found it amongst the books at Garvin's Mercantile. There were a few more we can think about buying, if you like this one."

She understood, he wanted to be outside, but this constant battle was becoming frustrating. She had a job to do, and if she was worrying about Andrew running about the ranch, she wouldn't be able to teach Tilly.

"Yeah, but—"

"Andrew, the men have work to do and so do you. You can't always be underfoot, and even though I know they are starting to pinch, those are the only pair of shoes that fit you, and you're going to end up wearing them out before we can get another pair made for you."

"I don't care." He folded his arms. "Stop calling me Andrew. I'm Andy."

He was being petulant, and Madeline counted to ten under her breath. Her brother was changing, and Madeline didn't know how to keep up. She wasn't used to this side of him.

He was usually quick to acquiesce, but he was already picking up some of Tilly's confidence. As the one looking out for him, it was trying, but she was also pleased that he felt comfortable enough to speak his mind.

Andy. She still wasn't used to the new moniker. Gideon probably expected her to be grateful he hadn't chosen something like Ace or Lucky.

"Let's just finish so we can do something else," chirped Tilly. "Maybe something outside?" She looked hopefully at Madeline.

"We'll see." It was more than likely she would agree, as the children needed to release some of their pent-up energy.

Tilly was pursing her lips at the pink tips of her fingers, when she decided to change tact. "Did you know? I don't have a mother anymore. She's dead. That's why she's not here."

Madeline froze. How was she going to respond to such a statement? It was hard to know if Tilly was looking to shock, or if she simply said aloud the thoughts that rolled around in her head. Was she avoiding embroidery with the guileless efforts of a child, or did she want to talk about her mother, and didn't know how to do so? Madeline didn't have any answers to give, but that didn't mean she couldn't listen.

"Do you remember her?"

"No, I was a baby, and babies don't remember much. We used to live in the cabin, but Daddy brought me to live here instead. He doesn't like to go there."

Her heart ached at the little girl's words. No wonder Gideon hadn't wanted her and Andrew staying there. It was the home he'd shared with his wife. The whole thing was just so tragic. What poor Gideon must have been through. What he must still be going through.

"My mother is dead. My father is dead," said Andrew.

Madeline began to panic that she was not going to be able to control the conversation. She wasn't expecting children to be so forthcoming over matters that adults talked about in hushed tones.

"That's double sad. Did you know them?" Tilly nodded but said nothing else.

"I guess," answered Andrew, his tone flat.

Madeline's chest tightened. She hadn't thought, until this very moment, that Andrew's childhood might have been much different from hers.

As a little girl, she had been paraded about with pride. It was only as she grew older that it no longer felt special, more like she was being displayed. When she came back from Miss Alcott's, she never thought about what it had been like for Andrew when she hadn't been there. This removal from Portland was providing her with a new perspective on their old lives. Her throat thickened as she looked at her brother.

She wished she could change things, but her parents were gone. They had done the best they could within the world they inhabited; pointing fingers and placing blame now was pointless.

"Do you look like your mother?" asked Tilly. "Auntie Emma and Teresa say I look just like mine."

"She must have been very beautiful Tilly. I'm sure your father misses her very much."

Tilly shrugged. "He never talks about her."

Holding up the tangled mess in her hands, Tilly wiggled the needle and thread. "How long do I have to practice this? My fingers are getting so sore." She dropped the embroidery on her lap with a dramatic sigh.

The little girl changed directions as quickly as her father. This time Madeline was thankful for the shift in the topics.

"Maybe a little longer. You've only been at it for a few minutes. If you persevere, you will be able to give your father, even your uncles, a lovely handkerchief for Christmas."

"Christmas is months away!"

"If you keep stopping, it might take that long," teased Madeline.

Tilly's eyes snapped up and she grinned at Madeline's playful tone. "Did you have to do this at my age?"

"I had to learn all sorts of things. First from my governess, then I was sent to a finishing school."

"Finishing?" Tilly wriggled her nose. "That sounds awful, like it's the end of everything fun."

With the exception of some of the friendships she'd made, Tilly's assessment was rather accurate, but she wasn't about to admit that to the child.

"Was your governess pretty, like you?" asked Tilly.

Madeline laughed. "Thank you, Tilly, that's very kind of you. My governess was ... pretty in her own way."

"Ahh." Tilly gave her a knowing wink. "That's the lady-like way of saying she was ugly. Uncle Luke calls that a nice personality."

Good heavens! There were times this angelic-looking child was more cowpoke than child.

Madeline sucked in her cheeks; her gaze narrowed. "I did not say that."

"I know you didn't. That's what I said," agreed Tilly.

"We can't just say everything that comes to mind, Tilly."

"But how will people know what I'm thinking, if I don't say it outright?" Eyes wide, the child seemed truly perplexed.

"You can still share your thoughts, but you must think before you speak. It's important not to say things that are hurtful, or unkind about others."

"And that's why you didn't say how ugly your governess was. But you know she's not here to hear you."

Madeline had a feeling that Tilly understood exactly what she was saying and would be findings ways to *not* say things and get her message across just the same.

Deciding not to press the point, Madeline shook her head and prayed for patience with all the Harts that had entered her life. "I think you know what I mean."

Beneath a dark fringe of lashes, blue eyes sparkled up at her. The little minx! They may not be the deep brown of her father and his siblings, but within those twinkling depths, there was no denying she was a Hart. It was impossible not to be captivated by the child, and even wonder what it would be like to have a daughter like Tilly, of her own.

As the children finally focused on their assignments, Madeline found that, like Andrew, her gaze was drawn to the outside. She knew it was foolish and that it was never meant to be, but her eyes still sought out Gideon. She liked to watch him as he went about his business, and it was almost thrilling to watch the way he leapt on to his horse as if he were one with the animal. Each time he came into the house for something; coffee, change of shirt, more coffee, she found her eyes following him. If he were to ever notice, she would have been utterly humiliated.

She really needed to quell any feelings that dared to

grow. It was hard to know when it started, but the moment Gideon gently brushed away her tear yesterday, she knew her heart was in trouble. His kindness in taking them in was only that, kindness. And he had only just begun to talk to her as he did the others on the Double H. Imprudent thoughts would threaten that. When Tilly said that her father couldn't even speak his wife's name, Madeline realized that he was still lost in a world of grieving.

Madeline couldn't conceive of a love so powerful. She could only imagine such a thing between the pages of a book. It was hard not be envious of the love they had shared. Watching Emma, and Micah, it seemed to be a Hart trait, to love so completely.

Distracted from her reverie by movement outside the window, she saw the very man inundating her thoughts, approaching the house.

"Gideon!" Andrew jumped up from his seat.

What timing. Hopefully her wayward thoughts weren't written all over her face. If Gideon Hart even caught a whiff of how much she was softening towards him, she and Andrew would be on the first wagon back to town.

Smoothing down the folds of her skirt, she waited a moment then left the parlour, nearly colliding with him as he came around the corner.

"Madeline ... hello."

Any welcome she offered was drowned out by Tilly's shouts as she launched herself into his arms. His daughter looked so small now, wrapped in his strong embrace. His eyes closed as he squeezed Tilly tightly. Then he gently released her.

Hand pressed to her chest, Madeline wondered if her either of her parents had ever loved them so purely as this.

"Hey there, Andy." Acknowledging Andrew, Gideon took

off his hat, holding his daughter's small hand in his other, and addressed the children. "You mind if I take your teacher for a minute?" He glanced at Madeline. "That's if you can spare the time."

Permission granted by the grateful children, Gideon led her towards the front porch. As he closed the door behind him, a thumping began in her chest. Was something wrong?

She waited for him to speak.

"I wanted to talk to you about Andy," said Gideon.

Oh no. She swallowed, her throat suddenly dry. "Yes?"

Toeing at the wooden boards, he answered. "Listen. Since you got a little fired up over the whole riding thing, I thought I better check with you first before I got him—"

"I told you, I won't have him shooting anything."

Gideon frowned. "There you go, assuming things again." He rubbed at the back of his neck. "What I was trying to get out was that I have, well ... a gift of sorts for him."

"A gift? What kind of gift?"

What was he up to? She hated that she was so suspicious. Gideon had been nothing but kind to them.

He bit his bottom lip, lifted a brow, then gave her a half smile.

"A four-legged kind of gift." He nodded over to one of the corrals. "She's waiting over there."

Madeline wasn't sure of what she heard. Was he trying to tell her he was giving her brother a horse? Why would he do such a thing? He was under no obligation to Andrew. Letting him be near the Double H's horses was more than gift enough.

He lowered his brow at her expression. "Now, hear me out. You said ol' Blaze was too big for him—"

"I never meant you should get him a horse!"

"I know that, but you were right, and Norval Jensen had

a little Mustang at his place. He wasn't using her. She's broke, and real sweet, and I picked her up about an hour ago."

Every muscle she had felt frozen. Including her tongue. She didn't know what to say.

"Anyway, I figured a cowboy ought to have his own horse."

Finding her voice, Madeline protested. "But he's not a real cowboy, Gideon. I don't know if he's ready for that."

Smirking, Gideon raised an eyebrow. "You better not tell him that. Besides, Tilly has a pony, only seems fair."

Who was this man who hardly knew them, but was treating them like family? It was a far cry from the man she'd first seen in town. Didn't he realize his actions were making it so they would never want to leave?

"Gideon," she whispered, looking back to the window into the parlour, trying to ignore the two faces pressed against the windowpane. "It's too much. Kind, but too generous. Everything you have given us is more than enough. I can't accept such a gift."

"It's not for you. Boy needs a horse, and that's one thing we have plenty of here."

His lips were pressed into such a fine line, that Madeline didn't dare to point out that the horse in question had only become Double H property today.

"Gideon—"

"Let him have it, Maddie. Please."

His fingertips touched hers, as he stared into her eyes, then he pulled them back to his side. Her heart quickened at his touch. Any protest she thought to make crumbled to dust. His humble entreaty touched her soul, and the use of Andrew's pet name for her left her fighting tears that threatened to fall. It would be much better if he wasn't this kind. There was no choice.

"Yes."

"Thank you."

"Thank you," Madeline countered with a quick nod.

And just like that, the moment passed, and a conspiratorial glint flickered in his eyes. Very much like the one she'd just seen from his daughter. The apple did not fall far from the tree after all.

"When would you like to—?"

"Now," Gideon broke in with a grin. He was like an excited schoolboy, and it was impossible not to smile back. "All right?"

"Yes."

"Tilly! Andy!" he hollered, as if the children weren't spying out the window. "Get out here."

They must have thought they were in trouble, as both scrambled out the door wide-eyed.

"Come with me," growled Gideon. She could see he was biting the inside of his lip, but by crossing his arms and frowning at the children, he looked formidable. If she hadn't seen him almost giddy a moment earlier, she too would have been nervous.

Andrew swallowed hard and grabbed Tilly's hand, who gave it a squeeze. As sweet as it was to see the reassuring gesture, and the alliance they had formed, she wondered if Gideon was taking this too far.

Nodding, he started walking. "You too, Madeline," he called over his shoulder.

The children trailed after him like little ducklings, trying to keep up with his long strides. She popped back into the cabin to grab the sunbonnet Teresa had given her the day before. Then she too scurried after Gideon, knowing that once Andrew got over the fright Gideon was giving them, he was going to be over the moon. Madeline didn't want to miss a moment.

"STAY THERE," said Gideon.

Tilly and Andy climbed onto the rails of the corral, and Gideon could feel their stares on his back as he was walking away. He had to restrain himself from running into the barn, he was so excited to show Andy the little mustang. Tilly had begged to sleep in the barns, the day she got her pony, and Gideon had a feeling Andrew was going to be one happy kid.

When Early mentioned that old man Jensen had been looking to sell the mustang, Gideon knew it would be a perfect fit. He was expecting his brothers to tease him when he rode in with the little horse, but not one man said a single word. He thought they would accuse him of cozying up to Madeline, and he was ready to tell his brothers where they could stick their opinions, but no one said a thing. Not that it was a big deal anyway. This was a ranch, it was chock full of horses, one more for Andy wasn't hurting anything.

Leading the horse back to the corral, Gideon tried to keep a silly grin from his face. It wasn't often these days he did something just for the pleasure of it.

Tilly was the first to see him, she went from curious to ecstatic quicker than a jackrabbit on the run.

"Ooh! Daddy! She's so pretty!" squealed Tilly.

Andy looked around the bouncing Tilly and saw the mustang for the first time. Craning his neck to get a better look, his eyes grew bigger as Gideon got closer. A warmth spread through Gideon at the boy's reaction.

Once inside the corral, Gideon smiled over to them. "Come on over, it's fine, she's broke."

Both children scrambled over the rails, and then slowed down as they approached the mustang.

Tilly was already scratching its withers, but Andy stood back taking it all in, waiting.

"She's not big. Can I scratch her, too?"

"Of course," replied Gideon. "She's real friendly."

Andy joined Tilly and smoothed his hand down the length of the mustang's coat. Already the boy seemed less nervous around this horse than some of the others and Gideon knew he'd made the right decision. Horses were big creatures: even if you appreciated their beauty, sometimes being up close could be intimidating.

"You like her?" he asked Andy.

"Oh, yes sir. She's beau-beau-tiful. The most beautiful horse here," breathed Andy.

"Almost as pretty as my pony," Tilly reminded him.

"I like this one, Tilly," said Andy. "She's—"

"Yours," said Gideon.

Andy hand froze mid stroke. His head turned to Gideon, as Tilly shouted her approval behind him.

Andy's voice was barely a whisper when he spoke. "For me? Really?"

"Really, kid. Cowboy needs a horse, right?" said Gideon.

He watched the boy fight back tears, as Andy looked across to his sister, then back to him. It was like he didn't know what to do next.

"It was your sister's idea. Blaze wasn't quite right, and this one here seems to be just about perfect."

"Maddie's idea?" Andy furrowed his brows trying to make sense of it.

Gideon wasn't about to give him all the details. He was

guessing that Madeline had been feeling a little left out of the new experiences her brother was having, and Gideon didn't want her to feel pushed aside any further. He knew what it was like, to worry the one you loved could be taken away. Besides, he wasn't telling a lie; Madeline had been the one to point out that he needed a smaller mount, and she'd let Gideon give it to the boy. No point in taking all the credit.

"Thank you. Thank you!" cried Andy. It had taken a moment, but the realization that he was now the proud owner of his very own horse was sinking in.

"Thank you, Maddie!" he called out to his sister, oblivious to the questioning look on her face.

"Come over here and meet her. Let her smell your hand, before you rub her nose. Lets a horse see you're a friend."

"I am! We are best friends," declared Andy.

Tilly skipped back to Madeline, dragging her over to join them. Gideon saw the tears in her eyes, and he quickly cleared his throat and looked away. He didn't want her gratitude, and he didn't want her thinking he was anything better than he really was. She would only end up disappointed.

"She's lovely, Gideon," said Madeline. "Does she have a name?"

"She will once Andy gives her one."

"Luna. I want to call her Luna." Andy softly spoke the name, holding out his hand out to her again; his hand not much bigger than her nostril as she breathed his scent in. Letting out a little whinny, she nudged at Andy's hand.

"I think she approves," chuckled Gideon. "She's a mustang, Andy. Smart little thing. She can turn on a dime and still give you six cents change."

Gideon could hear Madeline's soft laugh at his description, but he stopped himself from turning her way.

"She's a good little mare. Not a mean bone in her body. Reminds me of you, Andy. I think you two are going to make a good pair."

Andy threw his arms around Gideon's waist in a tight embrace and buried his face against his belly. "Thank you."

He wasn't expecting it, and he felt the men's grins and shiny eyes watching from around the corral, as he patted the kid on the back before peeling him off. Any longer and the boy was going to squeeze feelings right out of his eyes, and Gideon wasn't interested in that happening. He directed Andy back to the horse.

"Listen, you do have to watch her for one thing. She blows out when you get that saddle on. Clever thing knows what she's doing. You might have to tighten her up after about 20 minutes, but I know you've been working on that. Billy can help you with that. Right, Billy?"

"Yes, sir." The young McCarty boy hopped down from the rail and ambled over. "Why don't we get her ready for you?"

Luke already had the saddle ready, and Ben brought Tilly's pony over. Everyone was appreciating the brief respite from their duties to watch the excitement. Every man here could recall, in detail, the day they got their first horse.

Gideon retreated to watch from outside the corral, with Madeline still at his side.

They were watching the scene before them in silence, and Gideon took the opportunity to watch Madeline too. Her shoulders were relaxed and no longer up around her ears as she leaned against the rails, watching her brother and Tilly. It was a far cry from the panicked woman who'd been looking to skin him alive a short time ago.

Side by side, she was only up to his shoulder, maybe an inch more, so he couldn't see her face. Heeding his warnings about the unforgiving sun, she had taken to wearing a huge bonnet she must have found somewhere. It nearly swallowed her face whole. Normally Gideon didn't care one way or another about a woman's attire, but he'd quickly taken a great dislike to this enormous hat.

Not that he'd needed to remember what she looked like. Madeline was becoming fixed in his mind. There was no denying she was a beauty, and once again he wondered what brought a woman such as this all the way to Autumn Springs. The more he thought about it, the more curious he became.

He should just ask her. What was he waiting for? If it was bothering him so much it was better to have an answer and deal with it, than living with an unknown. He was about to ask, when Madeline started talking.

"He really likes you," said Madeline. "Hard not to though ... I mean, with the ranch and you giving him his own horse."

"He's a good kid. He's certainly taken to this life, and from the looks of it, the boys have taken to him, too."

A mixture advice, hoots of laughter and shrieks of delight floated towards them from the activities inside the corral.

"I don't know if he's ever had people so welcoming to him before. I think it's been hard for him at times. Children can be cruel."

"Adults too," said Gideon. "Too bad he didn't have a brother or two."

"He has a capable sister. But unfortunately, I wasn't always there. I was away at school, for a time."

He could hear the echo of guilt and defense in Madeline's voice and measuring his words carefully he responded. "I know. I didn't mean anything by that. Just that while brothers can be a real pain, they can also come in handy."

"You're right. I'm sorry for being so sensitive." She let out long sigh. "I've often thought it would be really wonderful to have another sibling." She looked up at him, her face peeking out from beneath that floppy bonnet. "Or five."

Her laugh was muffled, and Gideon was struck by a sudden urge to rip the hat right off, so he could see her teasing face.

"I would think that your short time here would have cured you of that." Gideon jutted his chin in the direction of Ben and Luke across the way. "What about your parents? Weren't they there to help him?"

She hesitated before she answered. "They provided for both of us. We were very fortunate. They did the best they could, in their own way." She paused. "It wasn't like this. You are very lucky to have a such a family. For all your teasing, there is no doubt of the love you all bear each other."

Her words stuck a chord deep inside his chest. Had Madeline and Andrew grown up unloved? Did that hurt more than losing a parent before even knowing them? Would Tilly have felt the same way if Cordelia was still alive, but didn't care about her own child?

"I'm sorry. That must have been hard."

Her hand waved his words away. "Oh, no. Father had his expectations, but he wasn't awful, and Mother was simply ... distant. They were never cruel, just distant, although to a child, I guess it can sometimes feel the same."

He wanted to reassure Madeline, hold her and somehow make it better, but he couldn't. He would only do the same thing to her. Cold and distant, because he was afraid to let the past to repeat itself.

Instead, he did what he always did, and pushed any feelings that were stirring inside back down into the little box that he had locked away deep within. It was better to keep it closed than endure any further heartbreak.

"Andy's doing great." Gideon kept his eyes ahead as he abruptly changed the subject. "Better than I thought."

Her head snapped in his direction, and his skin burned from blue eyes gazing at him. He didn't dare turn to face her.

"He is." She turned back. "You've given him more than just a horse, Gideon. He's coming into his own here. Thank you."

Gideon didn't want any more of her gratitude. He'd done it for the boy, not accolades from Madeline. This was getting way too personal.

"Well, if he ever wants to get out in those pastures and near the cows, he's better off on a horse anyway."

"What do you mean?"

"No offense, Madeline, but your brother's not a real fast runner, and the last thing he needs is a cow chasing him down and blowing snot in his back pocket." He could feel his mother's hand reach down from heaven to give him a smack upside the head for the crass description. "Forgive the colorful language."

Madeline stiffened next to him. "The reason he is running like that is because his shoes are too tight. You'll forgive me as I didn't have time to pack extras as we were flee—leaving Portland."

"Grab a pair from the house," shrugged Gideon. "There should be plenty of them. With a house full of boys, that's one thing we weren't short of. There's likely a pair in every size, somewhere."

She gave him a quick shake of her head. "Thank you, but those won't do."

"Won't do? I thought you weren't supposed to be one of

those, high-and-mighty city gals? Because I get a feeling if I ask Andy, he wouldn't be so picky."

He was almost sure he heard Madeline utter an oath beneath her breath. "If you must know, it has nothing to do with being pampered, and everything to do with Andrew's feet. His feet are wider than most, and he requires a custom fit. Although, I'll confess I didn't check Garvin's Mercantile, I assumed they wouldn't have anything suitable."

A knot settled into his stomach, and heat tingled at his face. Gideon wished he could take back what he said, but it was too late. He never even considered such a reason, but that was a point that Madeline was trying to make the other day. She was still his sister, and she knew what was needed.

Hoping to remove the foot from his mouth, he cleared his throat. "I shouldn't have said that."

"Well, you're consistent, Gideon Hart. At least when it comes to making assumptions about me."

Her arrow struck its mark.

Gideon opened his mouth to speak then snapped it shut again. At this point he was only digging himself in deeper. If he was worried that Madeline was starting to look upon him too kindly, he had certainly removed any chance of that.

That was a good thing, yet he was standing here feeling bad.

She pulled back the bonnet as she looked back up at him, her blue eyes piercing straight through his defenses.

"If the children are going to stay here, I think I will go see if Teresa needs some help. Some place someone like me can be useful."

She turned to leave, and he reached out to pull her back. "I'm sorry."

She searched his eyes, probably trying to see if he was

sincere. Finally, her wrinkled brow smoothed, and she answered. "I forgive you."

"Probably best you stay here anyway. From what Tilly and Andy tell me about your cooking, Teresa is probably better off without your help."

Her mouth fell open then snapped shut. Her eyes narrowed in on him.

Why couldn't he shut up? What was it about this Madeline Sheppard that had him acting like a schoolboy pulling braids? He'd only just managed to cool her anger, when he decided to start her up again. What possessed him to tease her so? Was it hoping to see that high color on her cheeks that encouraged him?

"Mr. Hart. You are ... you are ..."

Her lips pursed so tightly together that he suddenly envisioned his own mouth opening them up. An urge swept through him to pull this feisty woman into his arms and show her exactly what he was.

His body moving with a will of its own, Gideon pushed the offensive hat back from her face, and pulled her close, his hands gripping the sides of her arms. Madeline's eyes widened, and Gideon feared she could read every thought that was swirling around in his mind.

"Yes, Miss Sheppard? What am I?"

She put her hands on his chest; her teeth gently bit at her bottom lip.

If she meant to halt his advances, her actions were having the opposite effect. The skin beneath his shirt burned at her touch. His fingers tingled and the desire to claim those pink lips as his own was nearly overpowering.

"Incorrigible." Her voice was a husky whisper as it washed over his skin.

"And?"

"And I think I had better leave." Her voice was shaky. "Please."

Swallowing his need, he stepped back. He realized he'd gone too far. "I think you're right."

He couldn't call it fleeing, as she wasn't running, but Madeline took her leave as quickly as decorum would allow. After watching her go, Gideon turned back to the corral, to see Ben and Luke both narrowing their eyes on him before they cut to the retreating woman.

If he had thought he was going to get away with his behavior, he knew better now. He'd acted rashly, unthinking. There would be questions later, that was for certain. The thing was, he didn't have any answers. Thank goodness the children were too excited by the new mustang to notice.

Looking away from his brothers, he turned back in time to see Madeline disappear into the house. Gideon placed his hand on his chest, still feeling her touch. He had thought he could control himself. He had thought that no temptation could override his vow to remain alone and protect his daughter.

He no longer knew what he was doing.

8

———

Gideon still hadn't spoken to her directly since yesterday. If he was embarrassed or confused by their exchange at the corral yesterday, he wasn't alone. She was too, but at least she wasn't avoiding him.

When he carried in the exhausted Andrew—after he'd fallen asleep in the barn next to Luna—and put him to bed, he never stopped to talk to her, other than to say that her brother was 'all cowboyed out.' Did he think she was so naïve that she didn't know what had happened? Madeline may not be experienced in the ways of men, but she wasn't a fool.

The hungry look in Gideon's eyes as he held her, had thrilled and terrified her at the same time. When he drew so near that she could smell his scent of heat, leather and something that was uniquely Gideon, her first instinct was to push him away. But as her fingers pressed into the muscled hardness of his chest, she only knew one thing.

She wanted him to kiss her.

Not one of those awkward attempts by the boys or lecherous old men that frequented her father's parties. No, she wanted to be kissed, thoroughly, by someone of her own choosing, someone who could light her senses on fire with just a look. Someone like Gideon Hart.

But what did Gideon want?

She knew he was dedicated to the memory of his wife. Was the desire she saw in his eyes only of the flesh, or was it something more? Did she dare to dream, or was her wishful thinking causing her to imagine things that were not there?

The fact that he hadn't said a word to her about what happened, could only lead her to believe he felt guilty about it, that he was somehow betraying his wife's memory, and that he was ashamed.

It was probably the reason that even with Andrew and Tilly tucked tightly between them now on the church pew, and the service about to begin, that Gideon looked like he wanted to make his escape.

With many heads turned their way, he had taken her elbow as they entered the church, ushering her to their seats, but she wasn't sure who it was he was trying to reassure. The man looked like he expected lightning to strike.

Since he insisted on sitting silently with a grim look on his face, Madeline decided to take the time to observe the congregation, rather than making any attempt to get Gideon to talk.

The bench they occupied also held Emma and Weston, with Micah and Nora behind them, sitting next to Ben and Rhett. Luke was ahead several pews sitting alongside a frail-looking, white-haired woman. When she asked Gideon who the woman was, he simply muttered 'Flossie Gilmore' as if that would be sufficient explanation. She watched the two of them for a moment, fascinated to see the usually unruly Luke attentively listening to the older woman, his features soft, a gentle smile on his face. It was a stark contrast to the wink she witnessed him toss to one of the younger ladies outside before service. She reminded herself to ask Luke more about the woman later.

With all the Harts gathered, Madeline easily saw why the men turned heads. And it was hard not to notice how many were turned their way. It was a little unnerving at first; she didn't know whether they were trying to catch a glimpse of her and Andrew or the eligible trio of bachelors surrounding her. It was probably a bit of both.

There hadn't been much time to visit prior to the service. They arrived just in time for a few hellos, then found their seats. She recognized some of the people she had met in passing on her trip into town with Ben. There were several smiles from new faces, and one or two unkind glances from some of the younger ladies. Madeline did her best to keep a smile on her face, no matter what was sent her way.

Thankfully, Pastor Woods wasted no time taking his place at the front of the congregation and soon Madeline was lost in his sermon. He spoke of fear, grief, and the importance of community. He shared that grieving is a part of life, and if you avoid the pain, the hurt, then you will never experience the peace God wants you to have.

The pastor's voice resonated in the small church. In Portland, there were far more people and much more pomp and circumstance when she attended with her parents, but this little house of worship spoke to her in a way she had never experienced before.

She watched as Tilly and Andrew shared a hymnal, and while she was feeling connected, Gideon simply looked uncomfortable. When he wasn't rubbing at the edges of the hat in his lap, he was running a finger between his collar and neck. When he continued fidgeting in his seat, Madeline saw Emma reach over and squeeze his forearm. The small gesture brought a warmth to her heart. This family's love for one another touched her deeply, and she wondered if she would ever know the same.

When the service was over, Gideon dropped his chin to his chest, his eyes squeezed shut. Then he lifted his face and gave an almost imperceptible nod; liked he'd been in a battle and was pleased to have made it out the other side.

Tilly was already dragging Andrew out to meet some of the other children. Gideon waited for her in the aisle. Offering his arm, he gave her a slight smile.

"Are you all right?" she asked as she took the proffered arm.

Gideon cleared his throat, "Yes. I always find it gets stuffy in here, not much of a breeze." He bent his head close to hers to whisper. "It's also nice to have attention directed somewhere else."

Whatever had been bothering him earlier, he had pushed away. The man was mercurial, to say the least. He obviously wasn't going to address their moment yesterday, and Madeline decided if he was going to ignore it, then she would do the same.

Looking up, she caught him smiling. "Are you using me to deflect your pursuers, Mr. Hart?"

"I wouldn't word it quite like that but having you on my arm does seem to be making them more hesitant. At least until the rumors are quelled, and they realize our connection is strictly professional."

Madeline wondered if Gideon even realized how his words might sting. "I certainly hope there aren't rumors flying about. It should be made clear that I am part of your household only as your daughter's governess."

"Don't sell yourself short. You've been great with Tilly," said Gideon.

At least he was appreciative. "Thank you. Shall we get some fresh air?"

Gideon nodded and quickly escorted her outside. The sun shone brightly in the sky outside the church doors. Leading her through the throng, he brought them to Emma and Nora, who were enjoying some shade beneath a dual-trunked black cottonwood tree.

"My, what a gentleman you are, Gideon," said Emma. "It's nice to see."

"I'm sure," said Gideon. "Although it appears Madeline is the one doing me a favor."

"For now," Emma replied. "You can't hold them off forever."

Nora gave a soft laugh. "Micah was wise enough to marry quickly. I don't know how you boys stand it."

"We can't. And speaking of running, please excuse me." Gideon headed to a wagon where Emma's husband was waving him over.

Initially, she had thought everyone was exaggerating, but seeing the mothers and their daughters milling about with obvious interest, she started to feel sorry for the Hart men.

"I thought these towns were filled with men," said Madeline. "No offense to your brothers, but I see plenty of men here to go around."

"These towns *are* full of men. Ever since Fitz discovered copper in his mines, people have been arriving every week, it seems. When Nora and I were growing up, there was hardly a girl to play with."

"Absolutely true. I had no choice but to be Emma's friend," teased Nora.

"How lucky for both of us," laughed Emma. She turned

to Madeline, continuing. "But there are a lot more women here than there used to be."

"They must still have their pick of men. Mrs. Durnford implied as much the first day we met."

"Men aplenty, yes. Men of means, not as much," answered Emma.

"Ahh, I believe I understand," said Madeline. "It wasn't much different in Portland. Pocketbooks and power always took precedence over anything genuine. As a daughter, I sometimes felt I was merely a pawn to be moved in a businessman's game of chess."

"How awful," shivered Nora. "I can't imagine."

Neither could Madeline, not anymore. Now that she had seen the joy Emma and Nora experienced in their chosen marriages, anything else seemed unacceptable.

Emma nodded. "It sounds like you had more than one reason to leave Portland. I would never have been able to accept anything other than a love match. I'm glad you won't be forced to, now."

Madeline hesitated, then decided to tell them everything. "My parents, well, mostly my father wished for me to marry. He felt I was taking too long, and he wanted me settled. And by settled, he meant finding a husband that joined business ventures, instead of hearts. He was trying to make it very appealing to the man who finally took my hand. He was so concerned that he made a provision in his will on the matter. If I don't marry by the time I turn 25, everything goes to my Uncle August. Which is why he will do anything in his power to see that I don't even have a chance to find a husband."

It was embarrassing to say such things to two women who had attracted men who wished to marry them for love and nothing more. It was hard to know if any affection was real, when her worth was tied so closely to her father's bank accounts. Emma looked like she was about to ask another question, when Madeline was saved by the arrival of Mrs. Durnford.

"Miss Sheppard!" she exclaimed. "I am so glad to see you and your brother were able to make it to church today. It was nice to see Gideon here, too."

"It's a pleasure to see you again too, Mrs. Durnford. How are your wedding plans coming along?" asked Madeline.

"There's not much left to do, except the 'I do's' at this point," the older woman jested. "I would have been just as happy to have Pastor Woods say a few words and be done with it, but Jasper insisted that we have a large celebration."

"I think he believes the bigger the event, the less chance you will have to back out," quipped Nora. "He's head over heels, that poor man."

"Wes told him he should kidnap you, marry you and be done with it," added Emma.

"Jasper Wyley wouldn't dare to do such a thing. Tell your Weston he will be rid of Jasper soon enough. It's only five days now." Mrs. Durnford patted Madeline's arm, then let go. "Which is why I came over. I wanted to be sure that you and young Andrew had an official invitation to join us. I assumed you would come, but I wanted to confirm with you."

"Really?"

"Yes, really," replied Mrs. Durnford. "You'll both come?"

"We wouldn't miss it for the world," said Madeline, her voice cracking with her response.

It was as though she'd been brought by stagecoach to a fairy-tale town. Madeline couldn't believe the welcome these special women had given to virtual strangers. Despite the trials and tribulations behind her, she felt blessed that the path she'd taken had led to this place, and the people in it.

Andrew had never even been to a party. He was going to be so excited. She glanced over to where Tilly and Andrew were playing with two tow-headed boys, beyond the church. The careful plaits she had put in Tilly's hair were already unravelling, but the smiles on the children's faces, and the laughter that floated in the air, filled her heart.

After Mrs. Durnford left, Emma and Nora brought Madeline to meet a few more of Autumn Springs' residents. She smiled and shook hands, and soon got to where any new names she heard would be forgotten as soon as she heard them.

Nora and a lovely woman, Elaine Stockwell was her name, were in deep conversation about a rash troubling Mrs. Stockwell's daughter, when Madeline heard her name from the other side of the tree sheltering them.

"Miss Sheppard is a fine-looking woman, Gideon. You're lucky to have found her."

Gideon grunted. "I assure you, Fitz, she's only at the Double H for Tilly."

"Ah, you say that now, but I can see where a woman like that could change a man's mind about things."

"Not this man." Gideon scoffed. "Trust me. Madeline Sheppard isn't the type to stick around a place like Autumn Springs. Not a woman like that. She's got no long-term interest here."

"Heh. We'll see, old friend."

Gideon had lowered his voice, but not enough that Madeline couldn't hear every awful word. A buzzing began in her ears, and by the time it abated, the two men must have wandered off elsewhere, as she no longer heard their voices.

How could he say such awful things about her?

"Madeline? Madeline?"

Nora's hand on her wrist shook her from her thoughts.

"I'm sorry. I think I'm a little overheated." Madeline wasn't about to explain that her distraction was the result of hearing the man she'd recently wished would kiss her, telling another she was hardly worth meeting.

"Would you like to get some refreshment?" asked Nora. "I'm sure if we find Emma she would join us."

"That would be lovely, thank you," she replied. Anything was better than sitting here stewing over what Gideon said.

"Do you mind if I join you both?" asked Elaine. She gestured over to where her boys were playing with Tilly and Andrew. "I'm starved for female companionship, and I'm not ready to take those rascals home. Not yet."

"Of course," laughed Nora. "Completely understandable. I'm sure Madeline doesn't mind the break too." She smiled at her. "Elaine, if you give me Stephanie, then you will have both hands free, and I can get some snuggles in."

"Perfect."

The three of them went off to find Emma, and Madeline watched as Nora held the dimpled toddler, giving her a crush of kisses. Micah and Nora didn't have any children of their own yet, but there was a longing on Nora's face that pulled at Madeline's heart. It certainly wasn't her place to ask, but if Nora did want little ones of her own, Madeline sent a little prayer that it would happen soon.

It was a gentle reminder that everyone had their own cross to bear. She shouldn't be complaining, now that she and Andrew were safe. However, she was still upset, or rather more hurt, that Gideon would say such things about her. He truly was the most confusing man she had ever met.

When they were face to face, she was sure she saw the

same interest she felt reflected in his eyes; but his words told a different story. At least the ones he spoke to others. Not that it mattered. If he wasn't interested, that was the end of it. She wouldn't make a fool of herself fawning over him.

He was good to Andrew, generous and kind, and what more could she ask from a man who had said from the beginning that he wanted clear lines between them? He was holding up his end of the bargain, now she needed to hold up hers. He wasn't looking for a new wife, or even a new friend. He'd hired a governess, and that was exactly what she'd be.

AFTER HELPING Wes haul some wood to the back of the church for the pastor, Gideon took a moment to watch Emma, Nora, Elaine and Madeline chatting away. She certainly seemed to be making herself at home. In the span of a week, she already looked thick as thieves with his sister and Micah's wife.

If there were any whispers or gossip surrounding Madeline's employment at the Double H, people were keeping it to themselves. He'd seen a few questioning looks from some of the older ladies in the congregation, but as word spread that she was only another employee, and charged with Tilly, it had mostly been relieved faces. Gideon wasn't sure if it was because his daughter's behavior had the town that concerned, or that Madeline wasn't taking an eligible bachelor out of the Autumn Springs marriage pool. Although, looking at the antics taking place behind him with Tilly, Andrew and the Stockwell boys, he realized it really could be either reason.

Hoping to convince his family to head back to the

Double H before social invites were handed out, Gideon was on his way to collect his brothers when Pastor Woods called him. He was a good man but was the last person Gideon wanted to speak with. As the pastor got closer, Gideon needed to remind himself to relax his shoulders.

"Gideon! It was so good to see you beside Tilly today. I'm sure she was happy to have her father with her this week."

The pastor wasn't really being unkind, but his words still added to the guilt that Gideon already carried.

"Yeah, Mendo has things under control, so I was able to get away this time." Gideon wanted to be clear, that his appearance today was not an indicator of future attendance.

"Ah. Is Virgil Lamb still providing services to your men?"

"Yes," nodded Gideon. "You know the boys have taken to calling him Glory?"

"Suits him, but I feel it's more appropriate for a man in my position to call him by his given name," smiled Pastor Woods. "I see you brought Miss Sheppard. I was pleased to hear she would be attending. I was worried about her out there all alone."

Gideon felt his pulse quicken as he clenched his jaw. If there was an insinuation in the pastor's words, he best come out and say it.

"She's not alone. Miss Sheppard *and her brother* have been a real help with Tilly. You know my ranch hands are all decent men, Pastor. To a man," he emphasized. "Miss Sheppard is under my protection, and I take that very seriously."

"I know. Your brothers? I feel it's my duty to ask."

"My brothers?" Gideon almost laughed. "I can guarantee that there's not a single Hart looking for love," Gideon hoped his message was clear.

The pastor smiled. "Every heart needs love, Gideon."

Gideon shook his head and gave a low appreciative chuckle. "Very clever, Pastor."

"I know that you would never compromise that young lady's virtue, I was more concerned with her reputation. She's new here, and first impressions are important. I'm sure you can understand that."

"I do. Truth is, I'm not even sure how long the Sheppards will be staying in Autumn Springs," said Gideon. "And once we find a good teacher, Tilly won't be needing her."

He wondered if the words rang as false as they felt. Tilly was already attached to Madeline and her brother. It was becoming more and more obvious how lonely his daughter had been.

"The Double H isn't in town. That's a ways to be traveling every day for learning."

"We'll make it work," assured Gideon. He wasn't going to tell the pastor that he had been thinking the same thing.

The schoolhouse that had been around when he and his siblings were growing up had burned down after a bucket of hot coals fell over and lit the place up. It never affected them, since his mother and Mrs. Bryson had taken over their schooling after that. Then all the boys, except Luke, had gone away for further education.

"Miss Sheppard seems like a lovely young woman. I imagine that if given the right motivation, she would make a wonderful *permanent* fixture at the Double H. That is a solution you should consider, Gideon."

One man's solution was another man's problem.

Gideon knew what the pastor was suggesting; that Tilly didn't have a mother to handle her education. Despite the hopes of the pastor and the rest of Autumn Springs, he wasn't aiming to change that. Least not until he had a whole lot more information.

"You're as bad as the women in this town, Pastor." He indicated with his chin to the woman fixing her daughter's golden ringlets and pushing her over to Rhett.

"I like to think my responsibilities include both heart and soul." The pastor had a bemused smile on his face. "But I don't think I need to worry about Miss Sheppard. When her work is done with Tilly, I imagine there will be a line of men looking to court her."

A surge of heat flushed through Gideon's body. His eyes sought out Madeline, finding her still with Emma, Nora and Elaine. There were several gentlemen milling about, their gaze on her, while she remained oblivious.

He thought he'd already handled this. There were a few men he'd bumped into who were curious about Madeline, but Gideon thought he'd made it clear she was not available. Irritated by their interest, Gideon let them know that she might not even be around for long, so they shouldn't waste their time, or his. The ranch was a busy place. The last thing he needed was a line of suitors on the porch of the Double H. Just thinking about it made his temperature rise.

Grinding his teeth, he was about to march over and let her know it was time to go, when Mrs. Durnford grabbed his arm.

"Gideon, my dear boy. How lovely to see you in church today. Isn't that right, Pastor?"

"I was just saying that very thing," agreed Pastor Woods.

Deciding that retrieving Madeline could wait a few minutes, he looked down at Mrs. Durnford, and gave the older woman a smile. Then he had an idea. If the pastor joined them for supper, he would see that Madeline was in safe hands. With the pastor's approval, any rumors would be silenced.

"Pastor Woods. Would you like to join us out at the

Double H for supper? Luke spends Sundays with Mrs. Gilmore, so he won't be around, and you know Teresa always cooks enough for an army."

Pastor Woods laughed. "You Harts *are* your own army. I thank you, but I already have another invitation."

"I wouldn't fault you for cancelling that offer," said Mrs. Durnford to the pastor before turning back to Gideon. "The sheriff and I have a few things to run through with the Pastor about the wedding. Minor details, but you know how Jasper is these days. Crossing i's and dotting t's. Speaking of weddings, I've invited your Miss Sheppard and her brother to join us. I hope that you won't mind bringing them in."

If he did, he wasn't about to say it. The idea of dancing with Madeline held its appeal but looking at the circle of wolves starting to close in, he also knew he better not let her out of his sight.

9

I n the days that followed her exchange with Gideon at church, and the conversation she'd overheard, Madeline made sure that all her interactions with her employer remained as professional as possible. If Gideon noticed she was more reserved, he never spoke of it, and he seemed quite content to fall into this new routine.

The Double H was a huge ranch, but for some reason, despite her best efforts, she and Gideon kept bumping into each other throughout the day. He would give her a nod, a wave and sometimes even a smile; but he was always passing by, on his way somewhere, and never stopping to talk. Exactly as she thought she wanted. But she didn't, not really.

With Mrs. Durnford's wedding tomorrow, Madeline was starting to realize how important it was for her to attend. As much as she was excited to partake in the festivities, it would also provide an opportunity to meet some new people and find out if there were any other acceptable positions in town.

She didn't have many options, but there had to be some

sort of work she could do. She wasn't without any talents. She could give piano lessons in town or help other children with their schooling. She still hadn't heard back from her father's barrister, but when she did, if she received even a minimal amount of funds from him, she might be able to start a boarding house of her own. Unfortunately, they would be paying for room and *board*, and while she could handily change out sheets, she wasn't so sure that she'd ever be a good enough cook to feed hungry, working men.

Even contemplating the idea of leaving the Double H left her bereft. It was hard to believe she'd grown so attached to this place within such a short time, but it already felt like a home. It was obvious that Andrew also felt the same way. It was going to be a nightmare trying to convince him to leave, once it was time to go.

And Tilly. The idea of leaving the little girl almost broke her heart. Tilly brought a spark to her life that Madeline wasn't sure she wanted to live without. The part of her heart that had embraced Tilly might never recover. The more she thought of leaving, the more she hated the idea.

She felt like she was tumbling down a hill, with no end in sight. The infuriating man was so hot and cold, that she hardly knew which version she would be meeting at any given time. So, what was it about him that pulled her heart to him? Why did a man who would happily turn her away, still draw her in? What was it?

His tenderness for his daughter, and his kindness to Andrew touched her soul in a way that made her wonder how she could accept anything other than that kind of goodness in a man, ever again. The obligation he must feel, as the head of his large family, must be a difficult one. She knew for herself, how hard some days could be. But as firm and strong as he needed to be, he was protective and loyal to each one of them, and he carried that burden with love.

It was something she had never experienced, and the allure of such love was strong. But even if he hadn't told people she wasn't worth knowing, Gideon had already given his heart away. No woman could compete with a ghost.

Gazing from the window seat in the front parlour, she saw Andrew and Gideon approaching. Gideon was carrying a sack in one hand. Tilly had come back earlier, searching for a snack before bed, and was now rifling through the kitchen with Ben. Stepping back so she would remain hidden, Madeline realized she was no better than the children.

She took another peek from behind the curtain before they arrived on the porch. Andrew's shoulders were slumped, Gideon had his hand resting on her brother's shoulder as he guided him to the bench outside, beneath the window where she stood. Opened so she could enjoy the fresh evening air, the aperture transmitted their voices clearly. She quietly took another step backward, trying not to be seen or heard.

"You're a young man, Andy. I know your sister likes to hover over you like a mama bear, but it's okay to try a few new things, and fail when you do."

What was Gideon trying to convince Andrew to do? And was it really necessary to insult her to get him to do it?

"I can't learn fast," said Andrew.

Madeline was already picturing her brother, his chin to his chest, his broad face close to tears, rubbing his fingers together the way he did when he was frustrated. She took a quiet breath and told herself not to go running outside. Maybe it was good for Gideon and his never-ending confidence to understand that life wasn't as easy for everyone as it was for the Harts.

"These things can take time," said Gideon.

"Everyone is faster. I'm too slow," said Andrew. The ache is his voice was tearing into Madeline's heart.

Gideon scoffed. "You think men like to cowboy because they're happy to be in a hurry all the time?"

"I don't know-maybe- no."

"That's right. Out here, life can be fast, and it can be slow, but everything moves at the pace it's supposed to," said Gideon.

"Mine's too slow."

"I don't want to hear that from you. Not ever. You hear me? Luna seems pretty happy to me. Slower says you're learning the right way, because that can take time. I've seen plenty of men who get themselves a horse, and suddenly call themselves a cowboy, even though they didn't take the time to learn to sit a horse proper or treat it right. That's no cowboy in my books. So, don't go comparing yourself to others. The only real competition any man has is the one with himself. The only question you need to answer is, 'am I better today than I was yesterday?'"

There was silence outside the window, and Madeline tilted her head just enough to see him rest his arm across Andrew's shoulders, his finger lifted, pointing west.

"You see those mountains over there, kid?" asked Gideon.

"Yes, sir."

"Well, let me tell you something my father told me and my brothers when things were tough. He said that no man climbs a mountain the same way. It may be new trail, or even the other side of that rock, but everyone takes a different path to the top."

"It's not fair, mine's harder."

"Maybe. But you're going to find a lot of life isn't fair. Know what makes the difference in a man's life?"

"No," sniffed Andrew.

Gideon let out a soft chuckle and the low rumble floated through the window and brushed over her skin.

"Then I guess I better tell you. The reason that some folks get up that mountain, and some never make it past the first downed tree in their path, is a willingness to try. That's called gumption, kid, and you've got it in spades."

"G-gumption." Andrew repeated the word, sounding it out on his tongue. "That's a funny word."

Madeline heard Gideon laugh again. "It is. Now, if you're done complaining, I got a little something for you here."

"What is it?"

"You done whining? Ready for a new day with Luna tomorrow?"

"Yes, sir."

"Good. You said you were worried about being slow, so on the advice of your sister, these should help speed you up."

Advice from her? What was he talking about? Madeline heard a thump. Probably the bag Gideon was carrying as they were walking back. She heard a bit of rustling, then a gasp.

Caution to the wind, she snuck another look. Thankfully Gideon's back was to the window, but Andrew she could see clearly.

He was jumping up and hugging a brand-new pair of leather cowboy boots. "Boots! For me?"

She could hear Gideon's low chuckle, the one that made her tingle to her toes. "Let's see you walk in them a little. No use holding them, you got to stick them on your feet."

Andrew must have sunk immediately down on the porch. She heard another thunk.

"They don't hurt!"

"Guess those will do then," replied Gideon.

From her vantage point, she could see that Gideon was still seated, and Andrew came over to stand in front of him.

"You're the best brother in the whole world, Gideon."

Gideon coughed. "Might be a man or two hereabouts that would disagree with you."

Madeline already knew what was going to happen next. She heard it in Andrew's voice. She didn't even have to look. Andrew's ability to love purely was a gift most could only dream of having.

Standing before a seated Gideon, he and Andy were about the same height. Her brother placed his palms, one on each of Gideon's cheeks.

"I love you."

It was sincere. Andrew meant every word, and as she listened, silent tears fell down her face. She prayed that her brother's innocent declaration wouldn't scare Gideon.

She needn't have worried. Taking a moment to clear his throat, he placed his big hands over the small ones on his face. "Back at you, kid."

Madeline leaned against the wall, as she wiped at her tears. From serious to joyous, she could hear Andrew hopping about on the porch boards.

"These fit me just right. That's so lucky!"

"Sure is," agreed Gideon. "Now go in and wash up. I don't need your sister blaming it on me when you're late for bed."

"She won't. She likes you. She smiles when she sees you ... most times, anyway."

Gideon coughed, and Madeline clamped a hand over

her mouth to stop a gasp from escaping. Andrew's innocent comment was bound to be misinterpreted.

"Well, I like her too."

Madeline held her breath; was he only saying that to be nice to her brother?

"Good."

"All right, get to bed."

"Can I show Tilly my boots first?"

Gideon chuckled. "Yeah, go on."

Andrew didn't even see her in the parlour, as he tore through the house calling out Tilly's name. Madeline didn't follow him, instead she took a deep breath and went outside.

Gideon was still sitting on the bench and stood up when she came out the door. He held up a hand. "Sorry for the yelling. He gets excited."

"I know. I heard."

The sun was starting to sink in the sky, but there was still enough light to see the sheen in Gideon's dark eyes. Was he as moved by the moment as she was?

"Thank you." She gently shook her head. "Honestly, I'm not sure what else to say anymore."

"Thank you is fine," nodded Gideon.

Madeline smiled. She had no idea what to say. Andrew had said more than enough for both of them. "I should probably get them off to bed."

"Okay." Gideon didn't move, he removed his hat, playing with it in his hands and worrying the brim.

Turning to leave, Madeline hesitated. "Why, Gideon? Why are you doing all this for him?"

For a moment he didn't answer, he simply stood there, looking at her, softness in his eyes. She waited.

"It's not just for him."

She waited for him to explain, but instead he ran his fingers through his hair and shoved the hat back on his head. He still said nothing.

Madeline gave him half a smile, then pushed open the door. She was half-way through when he spoke.

"I like seeing you smile, Madeline Sheppard."

Her hand froze on the doorknob, then she turned around. But Gideon had already left, making his way across the yard.

CLOSING THE DOOR, and plunking himself down in the worn leather chair, Gideon let out an oath. He'd waited out at the bunkhouse with the boys, until he was sure Madeline had retired to bed before he snuck back into the house, and to his office.

"Coward," he muttered, as he shuffled papers aimlessly about his desk, until he gave up and sat back with a heavy sigh.

I like seeing you smile. Had he really said that out loud? Dang kid had him all mixed up with those puppy dog eyes, and words that tore through any armor he thought he might have wrapped around his heart.

Gideon didn't want to admit it, but Early, Emma, the whole lot of them were right.

He liked Madeline. He liked her a lot.

He like having her here, he liked the softness and laughter she brought to the supper table and everywhere else she went. And he sure did like watching her laugh with that smile that could light up the night. She was sweet, and she was resilient, but there was also a badger in those blue eyes, too. Heaven help the fool who dared to threaten her brother. Hard not to like anyone with that kind of loyalty to their family.

Tilly liked her too, and that was easy to understand. Madeline was loving and kind to her, yet still instructive in the gentle way that every child needed. Love, with clear boundaries. It was clear that the two of them connected in a way he never could have imagined.

The thing was, he didn't know how to go about tearing down the walls he'd built around himself. Even if he did, was he ready to? Could he finally put it all behind him, or was he going to stay stuck this way forever?

Everyone kept telling him it was time to move on, but that was easier said than done. How could he guarantee he wouldn't repeat the same mistakes, when he didn't understand how it had all gone so horribly wrong?

Cordelia's memory still held him captive, and he didn't know how to release himself. He was still living in the nightmare she unleashed on him.

When his mind first turned to thoughts of starting a family of his own, there were few options in the area, so Gideon had to look farther afield. A recommendation came from an old school friend's wife, of a woman from Butte, whose family had perished in a terrible fire while she'd been away at school. She'd confided to her friend that she was in despair about the lack of attractive suitors in the city, and when Gideon's friend mentioned his young, eligible, land-owning friend in Autumn Springs, she jumped at the chance to meet him.

It was a whirlwind romance. Gideon had never met someone who thought he hung the moon before. Cordelia was effusive in her praise and made him feel like a king. He took every chance he could to visit her in the city, and when she declared she couldn't live another minute without him, he proposed. He was sure he'd found the perfect woman in his beautiful bride.

What a fool he'd been. Taken in by a pretty face and flattery, he soon found out how low his pride would bring him.

They married and Gideon brought her to live at the Double H. She was happy to be the belle of the town for a while, but soon, that lost its shine. He tried so hard to show her the beauty of the land he loved; that there was a wonderful life that they could share together in Autumns Springs, but it was to no avail. Nothing he did could compete with the excitement of city life. She wanted fancy silk and satin dresses, and parties that allowed her to dance until dawn. Not early mornings, calico, and barn raisings. He could provide her with the money she desired, but not the decadence she craved.

He'd been desperate for it to work between them. With men outnumbering women ten to one is some towns, divorce rates were higher than they'd ever been, and women like Cordelia held the upper hand. Gideon couldn't bear the thought of such failure.

When she asked to visit old family friends, recently returned to Butte to oversee their investments in the booming mines, he happily sent her, hoping it would relieve some of her sadness.

And it did. Cordelia returned with a spring in her step and a smile on her face that he thought she'd lost. In the months that followed, Gideon was ecstatic to discover he was going to be a father. He prayed that their little family would bring her the same joy too.

But he was wrong. So, very wrong.

Her disinterest in their daughter started within a few months of Tilly's birth. Gideon attributed it to the difficult adjustment of becoming a mother and did everything he could to ease her burden. His attentions allowed him to bond with his daughter, but it widened the gulf between Cordelia and Tilly, and him. She managed to put on a good show around the family, who suspected nothing untoward but soon it was only Gideon who cared for their daughter when they were alone.

As Tilly grew older, and no longer required her mother for sustenance, Cordelia began to invent a number of reasons to go back to visit Butte. Eventually, Gideon stopped protesting, since things were often easier with her gone.

Emma and Teresa were happy to help with Tilly's care, and while they must have wondered, they never questioned his relationship with his wife. He felt so guilty that his child and his family were being affected because he couldn't keep his wife happy. No matter how he tried, he failed. In his shame, he became withdrawn and angry. Only once had his family tried to speak to him about her, when Cordelia was away on another one of her trips. His reaction was explosive, and from that point on, they never spoke of it again.

It all came to a head upon her return from yet another trip to Butte. They were arguing, again, about her apathy towards their family, when Cordelia spoke the horrible words that echoed in his ears to this day.

Why do you care so much? You must know, she probably isn't even yours. Look at her.

He'd been so blind. Even if he'd been gut shot in the moment after, he could not have been more wounded. The hurt from her disinterest, her infidelity, her lies, were no match for the pain those hateful words had wrought. That Tilly might not be his was crushing, but it was also unacceptable.

He told himself that Cordelia's spite would never sway him. It was Gideon who fed her, changed her, and rocked her to sleep. Tilly was his daughter in every way a child could be. Nothing could change that.

Not even the truth.

As Gideon watched his daughter's slumber Cordelia packed her things, preparing to leave in the morning. She was going back to her lover in Butte. She claimed she was done playing mother and wife and told Gideon that it was up to him what he did with Tilly, but she wasn't taking the child with her, nor would she be returning for her.

In the early mist of the morning, she took an old buggy from one of the barns, and left the Double H for good, leaving her daughter and husband behind.

Shortly after, word came that the buggy had been found overturned, between the ranch and Autumn Springs. Cordelia was dead.

It was Early who discovered the accident and rushed back to inform Gideon before anyone else knew what had happened. It was also Early who buried Cordelia's bag in an unknown location on Double H land and promised to never tell another soul.

That day, Gideon allowed himself to weep on the shoulder of his father's old friend. Early was the closest thing Gideon now had to a father. Then, he wiped his tears, pushed down his pain, and filled the emptiness with the image of his daughter's innocent face.

The family didn't know of his wife's intention to leave her child behind, and they never would. Cordelia's secret would die with her, and Tilly would never know that she had been abandoned by her own mother. His daughter would only know of the tragic accident that had taken her mother's life. A mother, he told Tilly, who loved her daughter more than life itself.

But Gideon never told Early what Cordelia had said.

That another man could be Tilly's father. He couldn't. That was one secret that he had vowed to carry to his grave.

He would not change the past for the world; it had given him Tilly. But it had also left him vulnerable. He had joy, but it was accompanied by an underlying fear. That was what Cordelia had left him with. A child he loved so deeply, it was almost impossible to put to words, and the knowledge that at any moment she could be ripped away from him if Cordelia's lover ever came to claim her as his own.

Gideon looked out into the dark night. The window in his room framed the little cabin he had once shared with Cordelia. He was letting her control him even now, and if he didn't put an end to this misery, she would have this hold over him forever.

It was time for him to get on with his life, and if she would have him, he wanted it to be with Madeline Sheppard. Sheriff Wyley and Mrs. Durnford's wedding was tomorrow. He would have the chance to talk to Madeline, to find out if she planned on staying in Autumn Springs, and see if he was right, thinking she might like him too.

Knowing his meddlesome sister was going to be there too dampened his excitement a little, but not by much. Emma would be happier than a hound with two tails to know her scheming had been successful. Gideon let out a happy sigh. He was never going to hear the end of it.

10

The laughter rang out into the night, as couples swerved to avoid collisions on the wooden, makeshift dance floor. The rollicking music added to the joy of the festivities, and Madeline couldn't think of a better way to celebrate a marriage.

Mrs. Durnford, now Mrs. Jasper Wyley, was clapping along to the sounds of the fiddle and mouth organ, while beside her, the now permanently-retired Sheriff Wyley finally stopped worrying at his snow-white mustache. The wedding ceremony was a short affair: a simple exchange of vows. It was followed by a veritable feast for all the guests, with an assortment of dishes brought by everyone. When Madeline pointed out to Emma and Nora that the dessert table appeared twice as long as the others, they laughed and told her it always was. The happy couple had requested that a favorite dish be brought in place of any gifts and Madeline had gratefully accepted Teresa's help the day before, in making honey tarts. She was relieved when they disappeared as quickly as she put them out on the table. When she saw Nora, she thanked her profusely for the generous supply of honey she provided them all with.

Andrew and Tilly, along with some of the town children, were jumping and twirling about to the music, and the sight warmed her heart. Her brother had never been to a dance, or a wedding, and was making up for lost time in his brand-new boots. He had begged to sleep with them on last night, and only took them off when threatened with permanent removal.

As they rode into town, Gideon let her in on the sneaky way he'd taken measurement of Andrew's feet. It was the day her brother had been so exhausted that Gideon carried him to bed. He laughed as he described how easy it was to take the measurements of a practically unconscious Andrew.

Once they had the right fit, Rhett had gone to town to find Jonas Sampson at the livery, as he was also a boot-maker. Jonas wasted no time in adjusting a calf-skin pair he'd been working on to fit Andrew's feet. They'd even made sure they had a cowboy heel, rather than a walking heel that gave her brother a little extra height and improved his chances of staying in the saddle. Her young brother was now outfitted better than many cowboys.

Gideon could play at gruff and stoic all he wanted but his actions spoke of a man with a heart as big as the ocean. He might shrug it off, as if it wasn't a big deal, but Madeline knew better. It was getting harder and harder to deny that she was falling head over heels for the widowed rancher.

"The children are certainly having fun," remarked Nora, as she, Emma and Madeline watched the bustling dance floor.

"They are," Madeline agreed. She took another sip of

the cool lemonade, relishing the not only the tart drink, but the reprieve from dancing.

One of the ladies standing next to them, tossed her tawny hair back, and raised her brow. "That one boy, who's dancing with your niece, a little old to be frolicking about like that, don't you think? Strange boy, if you ask me."

"No one is asking you, Charity. Must you always be so unpleasant?" Emma gave the woman a hard, thin-lipped smile.

The woman gasped, her mouth twisting as she turned on Emma. "I was only making an observation."

"So was I," replied Emma.

With a pinched mouth the woman shook her head. "Honestly Emma, you may be married, but you haven't changed a bit. And you're certainly living up to that Hart name."

Madeline watched as Emma narrowed her eyes and tilted her head, giving what almost looked like a feral smile, her dark eyes unflinching. "Wouldn't it be nice if, just once, you lived up to yours, *Charity*."

Charity's eyes bulged, and then with a final haughty glare, she marched off in a huff.

"Lovely," murmured Emma.

Covering her mouth, Madeline hid the smile that formed there. Her usual response was to ignore awful people like that, but Emma said every word that she would never dare to. Once again, she found herself grateful for her new friend.

"Thank you, Emma."

She waved a hand in dismissal. "Her father owns the bank. That woman acts like she has a head start through the pearly gates. Charity Forbes is a miserable person, who likes to make others miserable too. Now, let's discuss far more pleasant things, shall we?"

"Ladies."

All three women turned to greet Mrs. Garvin, as the kindly mercantile owner joined them.

"It's quite a turnout."

"I can't recall the last time we had all the Hart boys at an event."

"True," said Nora, then she laughed softly. "I see every mother is double-checking hair and dresses this evening."

"Speaking of which, where are they?" asked Emma. "I see Luke. He's making sure he's danced with every female here, in spite of their mothers' efforts. Although I do love that he's so attentive to sweet, old Mrs. Gilmore."

"Gideon's over there." Madeline nodded in his direction. Then she wondered uncomfortably if the ladies had noticed she'd been watching him all night? His sister never missed a thing.

"Oh, yes." said Emma. "I'm impressed he stayed for the dance, although I'm not surprised."

"He doesn't look like he's enjoying himself."

Mrs. Garvin's observation caused all three women to look his way. Noting their stares, Gideon gave them a tight-lipped smile.

"Oh no," said Nora. "That was unfortunate timing."

"Let him sulk. If he's not asking Madeline to dance, he doesn't get to be bothered by those who do," declared Emma.

No one wanted a man who was the jealous sort, but the idea he might be a little perturbed wasn't all that awful either. However, her new friend didn't need to know that. "Oh, I'm sure that's not it," replied Madeline.

All three other women laughed at her reply.

"I know my brothers, Madeline. In spite of their best efforts to pretend otherwise, they are used to being top of the heap. Gideon doesn't like the competition."

"Competition? What are you talking about?"

Emma might have mixed things up. If there was any competition, it was the futile one Madeline was in with Gideon's deceased wife.

"It's not your fault," reassured Nora, with a smile. "A woman as pretty *and* unmarried as yourself in these parts is bound to cause a stir. This is the first time you've taken a break from dancing since the music started. Take a look." Nora gestured around the floor. "They're just waiting for you to finish your lemonade."

"I don't know about that," said Madeline, averting her gaze. Her cheeks were now heating from more than just exertion.

"It's true," Nora insisted.

Emma rubbed her belly as she let out a scornful sound. "I don't know why Gideon would think this was going to go any differently. Men are such stubborn fools sometimes."

Mrs. Garvin laughed, "It doesn't get any better with time, girls."

"He used to be a lot of fun. Not like Luke and Ben, but in his own way. I know that was years ago, but he needs to move on. The way he's living isn't making him any happier."

Madeline didn't know what to say. She wished that Gideon would be able to move forward from the past too, yet she felt compelled to defend him.

"To be fair, he has a lot of responsibility. That can some-times feel very lonely." Madeline knew it did in her case. So, it made sense he might feel the same way. "He's actually not that bad. He can be very sweet. You should see him with

Tilly, and with Andrew. I honestly don't think I've met a kinder man." She sighed. When there was no response, she looked up to find her wistful tone had left Emma, Nora, and Mrs. Garvin first speechless, then exchanging little smiles with one another. Was she ever going to learn to keep her foot out of her mouth?

Emma tilted her head and gave Madeline a thoughtful look. Then her eyes lit up. Madeline didn't have to have known her long to know that Emma had something cooked up. Tilly, Luke, in fact all the Harts had that same gleam in their eye when scheming.

"Oh boy," muttered Nora. She took the lemonade from Madeline's hand. "She's up to something. You might need both hands."

Madeline watched Emma toss an impish smile Gideon's way. She then scanned the room until her eyes settled on a handsome, blond man, across the floor, with a bevy of young ladies nearby.

"I won't be able to stand here all night, waiting for something to happen, not in my condition," declared Emma. "Come with me. You're going to meet our friend Fitz: James Fitzpatrick. He's an absolute gem, and quite the catch. Owns several mines in the area. He can be very helpful in these situations."

That was the man she had overheard Gideon talking to after church. "I'm not—

"Trust me," said Emma as she waved to the well-dressed man. "I know exactly what I'm doing."

That was what Madeline was afraid of.

"You do realize that blatantly ignoring her is more obvious than simply asking the woman to dance? Stop torturing yourself and go ask her. Other men are," remarked Ben, as they watched Emma leading Madeline over to Fitz.

"I don't know what you're talking about," growled Gideon. He didn't need any reminders to see how many men were hovering around Madeline. Any attempts he'd made to curb their interest at church had apparently fallen on deaf ears. She was out and dancing to every song the band played. He'd been waiting all evening to take her for a spin around the floor, but he wasn't about to fight for the pleasure.

Weston shook his head. "I do. My wife won't stop talking about it. She's determined to see her new friend settled. If you're not careful, you might lose more than a governess for Tilly."

Gideon angled his head toward his brother-in-law. "You too? You're as bad as your wife. Don't you have some fights to break up or something, now that you're our only sheriff?"

"I've promised ol' Wyley that I'll keep an eye out for any fellas attempting a chivaree tonight, but other than that." Weston shrugged. "Who knows?"

"You should be keeping an eye on all these men."

"I don't know any law that states a man isn't allowed to ask a woman to dance," poked Weston.

"I'm not talking about that." He was, but he didn't need these guys to know it. All evening they'd been getting their digs in, and Gideon was rising to the bait, every time.

"Not everyone's drinking punch or lemonade," he said. Hoping to change the subject, he added, "I'm sure you heard what happened at the new station at Flintsville?"

Weston chuckled, "Sure did."

"What happened?" asked Ben. Thankfully, his brother was always up for hearing any new gossip.

"Some of the boys got a little fired up after a wedding out that way. Took it upon themselves to grease up the railways so bad, that when the train came through, no matter how hard the engineer yanked on those brakes, that engine went clear past town." He was still laughing. "Good thing the rail isn't here in Autumn Springs yet. Still, you're right, I'll keep an eye out. Liquor and young men can lead to more devilment in one night than you'd expect."

Ben started laughing. "I would have liked to see that."

"Me too," agreed Weston.

Gideon let the two men talk, happy it was no longer his business they were discussing.

He tried not to follow Madeline's progress as she moved through the crowds, but the more he tried, the harder it became. She looked lovely, and it amused him to see she had decided to put her stays back on for the day. Gideon wondered if she thought he hadn't noticed she'd stopped wearing them at the ranch. While it might be the fashion to cinch in every inch of a woman, there was something far more appealing in the natural fullness of a woman's figure.

Emma was doing her best to make him jealous, and she was doing a fine job of it. Each time he watched Madeline's face light up, smiling over something clever Fitz said, he couldn't stop from gritting his teeth. He didn't like to think of himself as a covetous man, but with each laugh, his scowl grew deeper.

Women as sweet as Madeline Sheppard didn't come along often, and even less so out this way. It wasn't fair to blame the bachelors of Autumn Springs for their attention, but he still did. Ben was right, there was no point standing off to the side. It certainly wasn't making things any easier or him any happier.

Looking away, he noticed a man standing in the shadows behind the band. He wore a gentleman's clothes, but there was something about him that didn't seem gentle at all. The man reminded Gideon of a snake, ready to strike. In the dim light, with his hat pulled down, Gideon couldn't make out his face, but he sure looked like a man he'd seen in town earlier today. Strangers came and went in town, but most spent their time in the south of town, in places like Belle's Palace, not watching another man's wedding.

He studied the man for a while, waiting to see if he would move on. Following the man's gaze, Gideon realized it was on Madeline. Another admirer? Maybe, but there was something about this guy that was making his muscles tense. If he'd gone up and asked her to dance like everyone else, Gideon wouldn't have liked it, but it would have made him less uncomfortable in his gut. But standing there, watching her ... something didn't sit right.

"Either one you ever seen that fella before? Behind the band a ways."

Ben and Weston stopped talking and looked in the direction where Gideon directed.

"Where?" asked Ben.

Weston shook his head. "I don't see anyone but the band."

Gideon looked back to where the man had been standing in the shadows, but there was no one there. "He was just there."

"Well, he's not there now," said Ben. "Quit looking for reasons not to ask Madeline to dance."

"I'm not. There was something about him. I don't know, I didn't like the look of him," said Gideon, frowning.

"I'll keep an eye out," Weston assured him.

Ben scoffed. "You don't like the look of any man here tonight. Do us all a favor: go ask Madeline to dance or head home. I can bring her and Andy back."

Did Ben seriously think he would just leave Madeline here?

Gideon let out a low growl. "Fine."

Fitz was one thing, but the thought of the man he'd seen, slipping through the crowd to get closer to Madeline was another. It was enough impetus to spur him to action. Sidestepping the eager mothers as he stepped onto the dance floor, Gideon reached Madeline, and stepped in between her and William Bishop.

"Miss Sheppard, may I have a moment?"

"I was just offering Miss Sheppard some refreshment."

Gideon turned, and Bishop stepped back. The bank teller was new to town, and seemed a decent sort, but right now he wasn't interested in soothing the man's pride.

"I think the lady is fine for the moment."

Bishop mumbled a response, and then with a rueful smile at Madeline he walked away with a heavy sigh.

"That was a bit heavy handed. Even for you. Is everything okay?" She swung her gaze to the dance floor. "The children?"

"They're fine." He gently cupped her elbow and led her to the middle of the floor.

"Did you want to ask me to dance, Gideon?"

What he wanted to do, was whisk her back to the Double H, away from everyone, and everything. As that wasn't an option, she was going to remain in his arms, until they were all ready to leave.

"It seems the popular thing to do tonight."

She frowned. "Perhaps, I should find another partner."

Before she could walk away, Gideon pulled her into his arms, he held her close, their bodies touching. They stayed like that for a moment, then he stepped back.

"Perhaps not," he whispered. He gave her no chance to recover as he once again took her in his arms, this time at an acceptable distance, and began to move them to the music.

11

───────

I t was a good thing that Gideon was holding her firmly, because the moment he whispered in her ear, her knees went weak.

She didn't speak. His dark eyes were locked on hers, as though a single-minded focus, and even if she'd wanted to, she could not look away. As the band played on, his strong arm pulled her into a deeper embrace, and her body melded to his, as if they were one. The rhythm of the music guided their movements, and Madeline no longer knew if there was anyone else dancing around them.

The moment was suddenly broken, when Gideon was forced to twirl her to the side, narrowly avoiding another couple. He didn't let her stray far for long.

As he pulled her back into his arms, Gideon broke their silence. "You're a good dancer. Although I shouldn't be surprised."

Did she dare to tell him that being held in his arms as he spun her about the floor was more enjoyable than any other dance she'd had before? Did men even want to be complimented on their dancing skill?

The corner of her mouth twitched. "Thank you. That's one thing at least I can thank finishing school for."

"I'm sure there are other things too."

"Not many practical ones," she smiled.

"While I hear your cooking is still...in discovery, you're certainly putting patience to use," reminded Gideon.

He was mocking her culinary skills. Did he not see how quickly her honey tarts disappeared? Or did he know that it was mostly Teresa's efforts that made them edible? Well, two could play that game.

"Oh, Gideon. Don't be so hard on yourself. You haven't been *that* terrible."

"I was talking about my daughter."

"I know." She gave him a teasing wink, and Gideon nearly stumbled. He caught himself and turned them in time to avoid a wayward elbow from a fellow dancer.

Gideon gave her a grudging tilt of his head as he smiled. "You are full of surprises, Madeline."

A surge of triumph shot through her. It was silly, and she didn't know where she got the courage to wink at the man, but seeing his response let her know she had won that round. Whatever game they were playing, Madeline found herself enjoying it immensely.

"Did you enjoy the wedding?" she asked.

"As much as one can, crammed into a church with the entire town, and few windows allowing a breeze," replied Gideon, his smile opposing his complaint.

"It was rather stifling, I'll admit, but they both looked so happy. I guess love can enter our lives at any time. It's never too late."

Realizing how that might have sounded, Madeline quickly looked away. If she thought he would let the moment pass, avoid it, the way he usually did, she was wrong.

Lowering his head, to meet her eyes, he lifted her chin to look up at him. He searched her face before answering. "I believe you're right."

Her chest was pounding so hard, she was sure Gideon could hear over the music. She didn't dare to dream, but something felt different. The stiffness that Gideon carried in his shoulders when he was normally in her presence was gone. The wariness in his eyes replaced with a calm that lightened his expression considerably.

The music stopped, but Gideon didn't let her go. He waited, ignoring the eyes that were turned their way, and once the next song began, he moved once more.

From the corner of her eye, Madeline could see Emma, Nora and the other Harts, watching their progression on the dance floor. Emma looked exhausted, yet absolutely elated, and Madeline imagined Gideon's sister was sure her meddling efforts were ending in success.

Did she dare to hope that Emma was right?

CONCENTRATING on the music and the woman in his arms, Gideon let himself enjoy the moment. He felt that he was releasing the chains that had held him back. He savored the gentle touch of her hand clasped in his. Their bodies were close enough to feel the heat between them. He let his feet lead the way, in rhythm with the music.

Holding her felt better than he could have imagined. The weight of her body in his arms, the smile on her face, that reached all the way to her eyes. Her teasing wink surprised him, nearly stopping him midstride, and the satisfied look on her face afterward, was one he wished to see again.

She was lovely.

Madeline wasn't wearing her hair back in the elaborate style he'd first seen her with, or in the thick rolled braids and buns she tucked up beneath that floppy bonnet he'd grown to hate. No, tonight the raven curls that she had descending from her simple bun to frame her face, were like glossy waves, the silky strands swaying in time to the music upon her full bosom, a few rogue pieces sticking to the glow on her neck.

Gideon immediately pushed away the image coming to mind, fearing it would be written across his face. The last time he'd let that happen, Madeline had fled at almost a full run, and Gideon didn't want her to leave his arms, not yet.

Looking into her eyes wasn't helping either. She stared up at him from beneath a dark fringe of lashes with eyes a shade of blue they hadn't made a name for yet. When high-lighted by the flush in her cheeks from dancing, a man was at risk of being lost in them forever.

"You look...different, tonight." Gideon traced her face with his eyes.

She lifted the thumb of her hand resting on his shoulder and gently brushed it along his jaw. "And you shaved."

A tremor ran through him at her touch.

"It seemed the thing to do. It is a wedding, after all."

"All of you look very handsome tonight, Gideon. I can see why the ladies of Autumn Springs are all taken with the Hart men."

Gideon wasn't sure if he believed it was the lack of stub-ble, clean pants, and a crisp shirt that drew them in, but he was pleased that Madeline had noticed. He should have told her how lovely she looked tonight, how watching her smile and dance was captivating, and killing him at the same time. That something in the air was calling him to her, and he didn't know how to answer. He longed to say the words, but he couldn't.

"I like to think we clean up well. Did I surprise you?" Gideon smiled down at the beautiful woman in his arms.

"No, a few whiskers can't hide a man. And after Luna, *and* the truly thoughtful gift of boots you gave Andrew, nothing about you surprises me. If Gideon Hart had a motto, I believe it would be 'expect the unexpected.'"

"*Inopinatum expectes.*"

Her eyes widened at his perfect Latin, and she rewarded him with a smile. "Thank you for proving my point."

"Education has always been important to my family," said Gideon.

"There are several words I could use to describe you, but uneducated would never be one of them."

Gideon spun her around, and then slowed their progress across the floor and lowered his voice. "And what might those words be, Miss Sheppard?"

"If you must know, *Mr. Hart*, I would start with 'dedicated father', 'loyal to family', 'tall ...'" A twinkle sparked in her eyes as she continued. "Stubborn and—"

"Stubborn!"

He pulled her tightly to his chest and he heard the exhalation as her breath left her chest. She was so close; too close, if anyone was watching. And they probably were.

She lifted her chin to stare up at him, her eyes never leaving his for a moment. She whispered, "Strong."

This time it was his breath that caught. Not trusting himself, he released her into a twirl and brought her back to an acceptable proximity. He could still feel the warm, womanly curve of her body next to his, and he longed to bring her back in to him, and to feel those silken strands of hair between his fingers.

"You should wear your hair down. It would be beautiful."

Madeline averted her gaze and gave a little shake of her head. "It doesn't seem very practical."

"Some things don't need to be." Gideon pulled her in to avoid the crushing step of another couple, let his cheek briefly touch her temple, breathing her in.

She smelled heavenly. Cordelia had always smelled of flowery lilac water, a fragrance he had never liked. But Madeline ... she smelled like something he wanted to eat. It was taking all his control not to taste her.

Lowering his head down, he brought his lips next to her ear. "You smell like freshly baked cookies."

"Do I?" Her voice was shaking, and he felt a shiver ripple through her.

"You do."

"It's—it's vanilla."

That caught him by surprise, and he softly chuckled. "No wonder I feel so hungry, you smell like baking."

She blinked rapidly, her cheeks turning a pleasing shade of pink. "It was Tilly's idea." I didn't have any fragrance of my own. And as you know, your daughter is very convincing. It sounds silly, I'm sure, but—"

"It works." He took another long slow breath in as he lifted his head. "Oh, it works. I can see why you have been so popular tonight."

Madeline's eyebrows furrowed, then, as they released her eyes began to shine, and she started to laugh. Not the giggle of girl, or of a woman pretending amusement at each clever thing he said, but a deeper sound, one of genuine pleasure and delight. It was intoxicating. He let out a low rumble of laughter, matching hers. He couldn't look away, he couldn't get enough, he held her close and swept Madeline around the floor. The rest of the world seemed to fade away.

There was only her.

And there was so much more to her than he expected. Had he known all along that this would happen? Is that why he agreed to Emma's plan?

The truth was it didn't matter why. He had agreed, and now, watching her smile, her body so close to his, something in his chest loosened. Like a light penetrating the darkness in which he'd been hiding for so long. Holding her like this in his arms, feelings he assumed lost started to return.

In this moment, he wasn't thinking about the past, he was only hoping that this song would never end. When the band finally finished playing, she was breathless and he was dizzy, and neither of them wanted to move.

The promise he had made to remain alone was becoming more difficult to keep with every moment he spent with Madeline. If he gave in to the longing from his heart, would he be left picking up the pieces again?

He didn't even know if she planned staying. Would her love for Tilly be enough to keep her here? Was *he* enough? If he was wrong, again, and Madeline decided to leave, he wouldn't be able to hide it from Tilly. She would lose another mother, but this time he wouldn't be able to hide his failures from his daughter.

He needed to know if whatever she and Andrew had fled in Portland was behind them. That he and Tilly weren't a stage station and nothing more. There was only one way to find out, and that was by asking. There was no point in spending weeks wondering, when the answers were available if he only asked the questions.

"Would you like that refreshment now?"

"I'm not sure that offer is still on the table. I believe you did a very thorough job of chasing Mr. Bishop away." She nodded to where the banker was now deep in conversation with Charity Forbes.

Gideon let out a little chuckle. "I didn't think I'd feel sorry for him, but now," he shrugged. "Would you like something?"

"I think I would like to dance to one more song."

"You would?" His heart pounded, yet she brought out the rascal in him, and the imp decided to make another appearance.

"Perhaps I should get Bishop then. It would be the kind thing to do." He didn't mean a single word. Now that he'd felt Madeline in his arms, he never intended to let her go.

The gleam was back in her eye, as she pretended to contemplate his offer. Then she whispered to him:

"Perhaps, not."

THE SILENCE between them as they made their way back to the Double H was no longer awkward. Gideon seemed as content as she, to be sitting side by side in the wagon. The moon, still high in the sky, was lighting their way home, and Madeline found herself truly content.

Exhausted from a night of revelry, both children were fast asleep, tucked into blankets between the empty food baskets in the back of the wagon. Gideon's coat topped the pile, leaving him with just his dark cotton shirt for warmth in the crisp night air. When he'd noticed Tilly shiver in her sleep, he didn't hesitate to give her the extra layer. The little girl never even opened her eyes. The rest of the Harts would return home later, still enjoying the food and friendship at the reception. Just before Weston had taken a weary Emma home, Nora and Micah had invited everyone for supper in two days' time. Micah had missed most of the dance because of a medical emergency, and there was the possibility it would be the last time they were all together before there was a new addition to the family. That they included her and Andrew in their invitation made her heart soar.

It was strange, having arrived in Autumn Springs only a few weeks ago, to feel so much a part of this community. She couldn't imagine that all towns would have been as welcoming, and she was grateful that her eye had been drawn to the name of this place on the board at the train station.

In the past few days, she'd hardly thought about Portland at all. It was becoming harder and harder to think of reasons to miss it. There had been no response from the barrister since she'd sent her telegraph, and Madeline wondered if her pleas for assistance had fallen on deaf ears.

While her father's estate was significant, she found herself caring less and less about it. If giving it up meant freedom for her and Andrew, then it would be worth it. Madeline was discovering that riches came in so many forms that didn't include a single coin.

She glanced at Gideon, then turned away before he caught her perusal. That was another wonderful thing about Gideon. If he truly was thinking he was ready to move forward, and to take that step with her, Madeline knew it wasn't because of her fortune. He would be choosing her, Madeline Sheppard, for who she was as a person, not for the money her hand in marriage would provide.

12

Gideon walked into the main house to find Madeline alone in the sitting room. She was working so intently on a paper that she didn't hear him approach. He took a moment to watch her as she worked.

Her back was rounded over the table, her usual perfect posture forgotten as she concentrated. Her thick black hair was wound back up into a simple bun, and as she looked up from the paper, he could see the graceful curve of her neck. He also saw a long pencil-lead smear behind her ear. He wondered if she realized it was there. He liked the idea that she had done it by absently scratching as she worked. Any chink in her armor of propriety made him smile.

He needed to focus, he wanted to talk to her about Portland. Clearing his throat, Gideon walked over to the table.

"Good morning."

Madeline startled, then glanced over at the clock on the mantle above the fireplace. "My goodness. It's almost noon."

"Where are Tilly and Andy?"

Watching her shoulders slump, ever so slightly, at her

brother's new nickname gave him almost as much pleasure as the mark on her neck. He chastised himself: he was being as bad as Luke.

"Outside, I believe. I'd given them some free time before we go on our scavenger hunt. I promised them since was such a nice day, that we could take a basket and look for interesting leaves, flowers and such, then create a book to explain what we've found. After such a late night, I'll be amazed if they manage to stay awake."

"Youth is resilient." Gideon nodded towards her drawing. "What's that?"

"A drawing," said Madeline. She didn't even crack a smile.

She was teasing him, and Gideon found he liked this side of her, a lot.

"Thank you for the clarification. I had always wondered what those were called. I do hope you are passing on such pearls of wisdom to my daughter."

A flicker of amusement ran across her face, and then she gave in and smiled. "I couldn't resist." She started to slip the paper in front of her into a book on the table. "It's just my rather poor attempt to capture some of the raw beauty out here."

"You like what you see before you?" asked Gideon.

"Very much."

She immediately realized the unintended innuendo of her response the moment the words left her lips, and her cheeks reddened.

"Really?" He gave an exaggerated arch of one brow. It was only fair he be allowed to tease her back. He was enjoying himself so much, he almost forgot the reason he sought her out in the first place.

"Yes," she spluttered. "The *landscape* here is much different than in Oregon. It's magnificent, really."

"Do you—"

He was interrupted by a loud crash and giggles coming from down the hallway, where Tilly's bedroom was.

"What in the blazes? Gideon scowled, turning to walk toward the source of the noise, Madeline jumping up behind him.

"Tilly!" he bellowed, "Get out here!"

Madeline coughed gently. "I've been trying to encourage your daughter not to scream for people. We've been practicing approaching, rather than hollering. Especially inside."

She was scolding him like he was the school-boy, and he realized if he'd had a teacher that looked like Madeline, he might well have been better-behaved. Then again, maybe not. He probably would have been too distracted to learn a single thing.

"Sorry," he said, then heading again toward the sound of the commotion. He was met by a red-faced Tilly in the hallway.

"Daddy!" Tilly pulled to a halt, narrowly missing him.

"What the devil is going on?"

"We aren't, it's not ... it was, ahh, Bandit. He knocked the chair over, and we were just practicing singing. Andy liked the hymns at church, but didn't know all the words, so, I was teaching him." Tilly was biting her lip, as she gave him a smile.

"And *you* suddenly know all those words?" Gideon crossed his arms and narrowed his eyes at his young daughter.

"Was that 'Rock of Ages' I heard earlier?" Madeline asked, joining him.

"Yes, Miss Sheppard. It seems to be his favorite. Andy, not Bandit, I mean."

Big blue eyes wide, Tilly tossed a bright smile at her governess. She had learned quickly at the knee of her uncles.

Gideon stepped forward. "Perhaps you and Andy would like to sing for Miss Sheppard and me?"

Tilly leapt to block his path at the same moment a strange sound came from down the hall. It was a familiar bleating.

"Is there something I should know, Tilly?" asked Gideon. He was beginning to get an idea of what was going on.

With a solemn face his daughter answered. "No, Daddy."

Gideon wasn't sure if Madeline was familiar with crossing one's fingers to cross out a lie, but he knew exactly why Tilly had quickly thrown a hand behind her back when she answered.

"Is Andrew all right? Perhaps we should check." Madeline started to walk around the pint-sized barricade.

Gideon reached out to touch her elbow. The contact stopped her in her tracks.

"Madeline, I think we can leave the children to their hymns, while we finish our earlier discussion." He raised his brow, hoping she would play along.

She looked from him to Tilly, and then back to him. "Oh, yes. Of course."

It was hard to miss Tilly's audible sigh of relief. "Excuse me."

In the span of a heartbeat his daughter disappeared, back to her room, leaving the two of them alone in the hallway.

Madeline shook her head, "You aren't curious as to what they're up to?"

"Very."

"Then, shouldn't we check on them?" she asked.

A very loud and purposeful "Rock of Ages" started up from behind Tilly's bedroom door, accompanied by some muffled shuffling.

Gideon chuckled. "I'm more interested in how they plan on solving their problem."

"Gideon, I think they have an animal in there and it isn't just Bandit."

"I think you're right. I have no idea how they got it in, but now that she knows we're here, I'd like to know how they plan on slipping it past us."

Madeline looked surprised, as though she had expected him to be angry.

"You're not upset? You're not angry?"

"If I shared even a handful of the antics my brothers and I got up to..." he shook his head. "A lady such as yourself would be horrified."

"A lady like me? I'm not sure if I'm being complimented or insulted." She pursed her lips, frowning up at him. "I'll have you know that I got into plenty of...things."

He wanted to laugh, but her defensive tone, and the look on her face made him think better of it.

"Let me guess—you switched salt for sugar at teatime."

He watched as her lip twitched in amusement at some long-ago memory. "Yes, just one of many pranks, I assure you."

"Yeah? You must have been a real handful. I'm starting to worry you're far too rambunctious to be guiding my child at all."

"You mock me, Gideon, but I can be as wicked as the rest of you, when I need to be."

Now, that he would like to see.

The idea of a wicked Madeline Sheppard was absolutely tantalizing. Since she was the very opposite of wicked, she didn't even realize how her words could be interpreted.

She glanced up at him. "Why are you looking at me like that?"

"Because, I—"

"You two might want to see this," interrupted Teresa, her eyes were twinkling as she entered the hallway, shaking her head. "I never thought I would see it...again."

They followed Teresa through the kitchen. She pointed to the open back door.

The cook gave Gideon an exaggerated sigh, shaking her head. "The apple does not fall far from the tree." Then she laughed.

Madeline exited, then walked to the corner of the house to look around. Gideon watched her jaw drop open, then she stepped back quickly, hiding from whatever she'd seen. Wondering what would have caused that kind of reaction, he peeked over her head to see for himself. She still smelled of vanilla. Any other time that alone would have been enough to capture his attention, but then he saw what Teresa meant.

"Are they really—I am seeing what I think I'm seeing?" Madeline squeezed her eyes shut, then opened them, taking another peep around the corner.

This was the first time he'd seen her utterly speechless.

Luke was outside Tilly's window, determinedly trying to haul a goat through the window. Bandit jumped with excitement at the pair, and they could hear Andy singing his heart out with the wrong words to Rock of Ages, attempting to cover the sound of the goat's bleating.

Like two eavesdropping children, Gideon and Madeline

pressed their backs against the wall, pressing their hands against their mouths, listening to the chaos unfold.

"Seriously, Tilly. How'd you get this, blasted critter in there in the first place? What were you two thinking?"

"Danny and Kevin Stockwell said they taught their goat to sing. We thought we'd get Percy to sing too." She was explaining to Luke as if it made complete sense.

"In your room?"

Luke sounded incredulous, and Gideon shook his head. Did his brother so quickly forget his own capers as a child? Or even last week.

"Yeah," Tilly grunted, as she tried to lift the hind end of the unobliging goat. "I wanted to show Andy how good Percy could climb. He got in fine, but now he won't get out."

The sounds stopped. Neither he nor Madeline dared to look around the corner.

"Tilly, you know letting a cat out of a bag is a whole lot easier than getting it back in. Same goes for goats. Let me grab Ben. Unless this stupid goat cooperates, it's going to take two of us," said Luke.

"But not Daddy, right Uncle Luke? Pinky swear?"

Luke laughed. "All right, not that old grump. But you're gonna owe me one, kid. Both of you. Hold tight, and don't let him mess on the floor. That, I'm not helping with."

Madeline let out a squeak, then turned her face into his chest in effort to muffle the noise. Luke still wasn't finished insulting him.

"Geez Louise, kid. Gideon's cranky enough as it is."

Madeline was covering her mouth and had tears coming from her eyes. If her shoulders hadn't been shaking with suppressed laughter, he might have been worried.

He pulled her back and looked down at her red face

with feigned injury and whispered, "Cranky? Can you believe that?"

Eyes dancing she kept her hands over her mouth but shook her head, with exaggerated disbelief.

"Come on. I think Luke has this under control. I don't believe we are needed or wanted here."

"Oh, Gideon!" Madeline's voice was breathless with amusement. "I can't ... you aren't even shocked?"

Escorting her back through the door to the kitchen, he said, "Welcome to the Double H, Miss Madeline Sheppard. It's not for everyone, but I can guarantee there's never a dull moment around here."

"Never was," added Teresa. She looked at Gideon and gave him a knowing smile. "Nice to see it starting over again."

MAKING their way to the front porch, Madeline and Gideon sat in two of the rocking chairs, waiting to see how events would unfold with the children. It was like watching their own comedic play, with no idea how it would end.

Ben and Luke passed by with a nonchalant wave. They rounded the corner of the house, then after a few minutes, and another rousing chorus of "Rock of Ages" from Tilly's room, the men both returned, leading Percy back to the barns. Neither brother said a word, but as they got farther away from the main house, she could see them doubling over in laughter.

It wasn't long before Tilly and Andrew appeared. Looking as though butter wouldn't melt in their mouths they asked if they could go to the creek and begin the promised scavenger hunt. Tilly implored her father to join them, and Madeline was pleasantly surprised when he agreed.

Gathering a basket from the kitchen and a bag, for each child's finds, they were soon off. Tilly and Andrew kept up a steady stream of conversation, until they arrived at the creek, and then, mid-sentence in a story, they shot off to the water.

Madeline sat on the spread blanket, the wind softly rustling the leaves on the trees above. She kept fussing with the basket of goodies they had packed, waiting for Gideon to speak, as he sat down beside her. This all felt so new and different that she wasn't sure what to say. Gideon seemed hesitant too.

They watched the children for a few moments, each lost in their own thoughts, as the sun shone down through the trees, warming them. After a late night of wedding festivities, Madeline could feel slumber creeping in. Her eyes were just starting to shut when Gideon spoke.

"Do you ever worry that what you're doing isn't going to be enough?"

That woke her up. Was Gideon talking about Andrew? Her time with Tilly?

"I worry all the time. I worry that if I don't make the right decisions, that my choices will hurt the people I love."

Gideon gave her a questioning look. "What choices?"

"Any of them, all of them. You have a daughter, I'm sure you feel the same way."

A burst of laughter and the sounds of splashing caused them both to smile.

"I do. More than you know," said Gideon.

His tone wasn't ominous, but it was tinged with sadness, and Madeline thought about all he'd been through.

"I'm sure it has been difficult for you."

Gideon sat up straight. "Why are you here?"

"Pardon me?" What was he really asking, and why did this picnic suddenly feel like an inquisition?

"You've never said why you left Portland. Maybe you told Emma, I don't know. But I want things to be open between us." He touched her arm, then pulled his hand back. "I don't want you to feel like you need to hide anything."

She wasn't hiding, not from Gideon anyway. There was no reason she should feel any embarrassment, she'd done nothing wrong. Andrew had done nothing wrong. Any shame should be carried by her uncle, not her.

"Madeline," Gideon prodded. "Why did you leave Portland?"

"I had to. He was ..." she hesitated. How did could she explain her uncle to a man who only knew love from his family?

"So, it was a man." Gideon's tone was flat. He seemed to withdraw from her without even moving an inch.

She sighed, "I should probably be insulted by the insinuation of your words, but I can't really blame you because yes, it was a man, but not in the way you think."

His cheeks flushed as she spoke, and this time he did move back on the blanket. "If you're running from your husband, you need to know that I won't be party to it."

Husband! Madeline's jaw nearly hit the ground before she snapped it shut. "I am not running from a husband—"

"Lover?" he spit the words as though he swallowed a mouth full of nails.

She almost slapped him. "Gideon Hart! I don't know what would make you even say such an awful thing, but if you stop interrupting for one moment, I can tell you that it's *my uncle*. Andrew and I needed to get away from my father's brother. Not some ... I won't even say such an offensive word."

He dropped his chin, refusing to meet her eyes. Good. He should be ashamed.

"Forgive me. I didn't know."

His sincerity only slightly diminished her irritation. "Of course, you didn't, but that doesn't explain why your first thought was to assume the worst of me. What on earth has made you so suspicious? The rest of your family isn't afflicted with such distemper."

"Distemper?"

"Yes. D-I-S—"

"I don't need a spelling lesson from my daughter's governess, thank you," said Gideon, as he boldly held her gaze.

"You could do with a few lessons in common courtesy." Madeline crossed her arms and returned gaze for gaze. Gideon Hart might have stolen her heart over the past few weeks, but he wasn't stealing her self-respect.

Gideon was the first to look away. He let out a long sigh. "Perhaps ... probably."

Madeline's shoulders lowered. She couldn't stay angry with a man looking so defeated, even if he deserved it. What was it that caused him to behave this way? She never saw him like this with anyone else.

"Gideon," she hesitated, then plunged ahead. "Is it something I've done? I've wracked my brain, hoping to understand, but I can't think of anything that would make you so suspicious of me. You know I would never do anything to hurt you or Tilly. She's the most wonderful little girl. I can only dream of having a child, just like her, one day."

Her words didn't seem to comfort him. His face fell.

"I can see how much you care for Tilly. It's not that."

"Oh." Her eyes met his and Madeline knew. It was her.

She'd been acting all twitterpated, and he felt guilty for his feelings. He probably felt the connection between them was a betrayal to his wife. She had hoped for too much too soon, and that was hurting him. She couldn't change what had taken place, but at least she could answer the question he had asked.

"I don't know why you agreed to take us in, Gideon. But I am grateful that you did. If we hadn't met your sister, I'm not sure where Andrew and I would be right now." She spread her skirts across the blanket, smoothing her hands into their folds. "It's no secret that Andrew is different from most other children. You have all been so welcoming, but that hasn't always been the case."

Madeline took a deep breath and continued. "Having a brother as special as he is has taught me about love in a way I wish others had the chance to experience. I am the richer for having him as my brother. My parents did their best, but once they passed away they left us under the 'protection' of my Uncle August." She almost spit the word *protection*. "Everything a guardian should be, he was not. He didn't want either one of us around, but it was Andrew who he first took issue with. Once he threatened to lock him away, I knew I had to make a decision."

Now she had Gideon's full attention. "Lock him away? What do you mean?"

"Exactly what I said. He has enough connections to do so, and no one would question him."

"But ... you're family!?" He really couldn't understand. That only further proved what a good man he was.

"I don't think you realize how unusual your family bonds are. Not everyone is so lucky."

"Your uncle doesn't even deserve to be called family, if that is what he planned. It's despicable. He's, he's—"

"Diabolical? Yes. But now he is behind us, because I did it. I took Andrew and myself out of there. I'm stronger than you might think, Gideon." Madeline gave him a defiant nod.

"I'm beginning to see that." There was a pause. "Does he know where you are?"

"No."

"Good. We're going to keep it that way. You and Andrew are going to be safe here. Always."

His face and tone brooked no argument, and Madeline really didn't feel like giving him one. She'd left out some of her story, the parts that involved her inheritance, and that her uncle August was willing to put her behind bars to ensure he got it, but she didn't think that mattered, not really. The point was, she would have left, if only to protect Andrew, and now that she was away from Portland and her uncle's greed, the rest didn't matter.

What if she *did* tell him of her father's trust and what the man who married her would stand to gain? Gideon might see her through different eyes. Would he still hold tightly to the memory of his wife? He was a wealthy man in his own right, but if there was one lesson she'd learned these past few months, it was that for some men, there was no such thing as enough.

There was nothing to indicate that Gideon Hart was that kind of man. The truth was, she didn't really even know how much she would inherit, other than that it was enough to make a greedy man do horrendous things. She didn't want Gideon to be drawn to her for any reason other than love, and if that were to ever happen, he needed time.

"Thank you, Gideon. I appreciate that. It's exciting to think that we might be able to start over."

"You want to start over?" He suddenly brightened. Did the man even realize how mercurial he could be?

"I do, and I can think of no better place than right here, in Autumn Springs. All of you, the entire community has opened its arms to us. I can't think of a single reason to leave."

There were two good reasons she could name for staying, and they started with Gideon and Tilly, but she didn't need to frighten him by saying it out loud.

He looked surprisingly relieved. Then he reached out and folded her hand in his. "I think that's fine, Madeline. You both deserve it."

"Thank you." There was so much more she wanted to say, but she remained silent. His promise to protect her, to keep her safe, was enough. It had to be.

He squeezed her hand and let go.

She looked away from him to the creek, where Tilly had convinced Andrew to dip his toes in the cool water, fresh from the mountains. He was so happy. She discreetly rubbed her eyes, hoping to stave off any tears that threatened. The last she needed was to try to explain why she was crying.

"Thank you. I'm glad that I've told you. I should have done so from the start, but I think I needed time to really understand what had happened. It all unfolded so quickly." She didn't need to share that she had spent her first night at the Double H, crying into her pillow.

"You've had a lot to carry," replied Gideon.

"Something I'm sure you can understand."

It hadn't been easy for him, and no matter how she was feeling in this moment she needed to remember that.

"I do," said Gideon.

Madeline waited for him to continue. She didn't want to

talk about herself anymore. She was afraid she would expose the very feelings she was trying to bury.

"It's not that I don't love my family. I do, they're everything to me, but it can be difficult as the oldest. It comes with an obligation the others don't have." He shrugged one shoulder. "That's not a complaint, just fact."

"True, and I only have one brother not four brothers and a sister."

"Only three left in the house now. They're all starting to build their own lives. I'll confess that I'm hoping they stick around. It's a family ranch, a huge operation. I want them at my side."

"I think that Luke and Ben will stay. They seem to love the land as much as you do," said Madeline.

Gideon laughed, "It's Teresa's cooking Ben loves most of all."

Madeline shook her head. "You all tease him, but can you blame him?" She swept her hand across the small feast they'd stolen from the kitchen.

"I guess not. I'm glad that Andy is taking to things the way he has."

"If you are referring to my brother becoming a full-blown cowboy in the span of a few weeks, then yes, he has." She smiled.

It was impossible to remain frustrated with the man when she thought of all he'd done for Andrew. The turmoil in her heart didn't change the fact that Gideon was to thank for all the wonderful, confident changes she'd seen in her brother. They never would have happened if she hadn't met him, and for that she would always be grateful.

Madeline reminded herself that nothing good could come of trying to force a person to want you, to be with you, to love you. It had to happen in its own time, or it would be doomed from the start.

GIDEON RAN his fingers through his hair, then gave a little shake of his head. "You know, at some point, you're going to have to start calling him Andy."

She wrinkled her nose like there was a bad smell. "That day is a long way off. He's been Andrew too long."

"I think you actually like it. I can tell by looking at you. I think you just don't want to admit you were wrong," said Gideon.

"Is that what my face is saying?"

"Yup, and my face is saying it's time to stuff one of those donuts into it." Gideon grinned and grabbed one of Teresa's powdery treats, swallowing it in two bites.

She shook her head in what looked to him like an amused exasperation. "And you wonder where you daughter gets it."

"Don't sell yourself short, Madeline. I'm seeing some improvements."

"After this morning's mischief, I'm not so sure." He could tell she was still contemplating talking to Andy privately about the issue. She claimed she'd been as mischievous as the next child, but that was a whole lot different than growing up a Hart.

That woodpile was always high when his father was alive, as nearly all punishment for transgressions included chopping time at the stump. The strength and size of each brother by the time they hit sixteen was a testament to a childhood fully enjoyed.

Gideon shot her a smile. "I wasn't expecting miracles."

"That provides some relief," said Madeline.

Gideon chuckled as he pictured Luke yanking on poor Percy, while Andy and Tilly repeated the first four lines of "Rock of Ages," over and over. He knew he shouldn't be so lenient, but he was glad she was still having fun. Time passed quickly, and she would be forced into propriety soon enough.

"For someone with no formal teaching, you're a natural with her. I'm sure she's thinking she's gotten away without learning a thing today, but I'm on to you. The scavenger hunt and book are a great idea."

Tilting her head back she gave a little laugh. "That's exactly what they're both thinking. She's really such a bright child. A joy to be around. I confess I'm quite taken with her. She has a lot to share."

Gideon watched Madeline's face soften as she watched his daughter and an unexpected warmth expanded through his chest. He traced the lines of her delicate jaw with his eyes, down to the stripe of pencil lead still evident on her neck. His finger itched to follow the path his eyes had taken, to feel the smoothness of her cheek.

She turned, caught him looking and his heart tripped as her cheeks bloomed pink.

There was a soot-colored lash below her eye, and before he knew it, his finger was pressing against her creamy skin, transferring the eyelash to the tip of it.

He looked at it, then offered it to her lips. "Go ahead and blow. Make a wish."

Blue eyes widened at the intimate invitation. "Gideon Hart, I didn't imagine you one for fanciful notions."

He leaned in closer, allowing himself to take in the faint smell of vanilla that made him want to taste her. "There's much to learn about me, Miss Sheppard."

"I expect that is true." Her words came out as a whisper.

He pulled back, still holding out his finger, the lash waiting. "Last chance."

Her eyes narrowed on the lash, hesitating. He couldn't tell if she was struggling to pick a wish or deciding whether to oblige him. She let out a soft sigh, closed her eyes, leaned in and blew on the eyelash.

His pulse raced at the feeling, and Gideon was thankful he was already seated as his whole body became weak. One tiny breath, and she felled him. Never in his life had he reacted to a woman in such a way.

"What—" He cleared his throat. "What did you wish for?"

"Am I supposed to tell you? Will it still come true if I do?"

"There's only one way to find out."

She tilted her head, as if weighing her choices. He was now more curious than ever. Was she embarrassed to say what it was?

"A chance to play the piano again."

This was not the answer that Gideon had been expecting. "A piano? That's what you wished for?"

She corrected him. "Just the chance to play one."

"Are you good?"

She gave him a soft smile. "Not enough talent for an audience, but I could make my way through the pieces we had. When Andrew was a baby, he could get fussy. Sometimes the only thing that would quiet him down was when I played for him. He loves music." Her blue eyes sparkled. "Apparently he has a special fondness for hymns."

Gideon laughed at the reminder.

"My mother played too. I never heard her though; she

couldn't bring their piano when they made the journey here to Montana Territory."

"What a shame," said Madeline. "Even now, it would be difficult to get one here. I'm guessing that's why the church doesn't have one."

"I guess so. I hadn't given it much thought," shrugged Gideon.

"It doesn't matter. There are many beautiful voices, and it was just a silly wish." She seemed embarrassed to have shared her thoughts.

"Maddie! Look!" Andy was jumping up and down, hollering and pointing at something Tilly had cupped in her hands.

Gideon chuckled at their excitement. He used to love coming down to this very creek with his brothers.

Standing, Madeline looked down at him, the sun a halo around her face. "If you'll excuse me."

She didn't wait for a response and starting walking away.

He called after her. "My mother."

Madeline stopped and turned. "Pardon?"

"My mother. She was the one with the fanciful notions. When any of us would lose a lash, she would tell us to make a wish."

Why was he telling her this? It wasn't important, yet he wanted to share it with her.

She smiled and placed a hand over her heart. "What a nice memory to have. I would have liked to have met her, Gideon. She sounds like a wonderful mother."

"She was."

"I guess that's why you are such a good father."

Her words hit him deep in his chest. Like a balm on an aching wound. She couldn't know how much that simple statement meant to him.

He wanted to say thank you, but he'd taken too long to respond, and she was already off joining the children.

Gideon leaned back stretching out his legs, extending them well past the edge of the blanket. Loosening his gun belt, grabbing his hat and tipping over his face, he thought he might sneak in some shuteye to the sound of the children playing.

But five minutes later he found himself still gazing from beneath his hat at the scene by the water's edge. Tilly was twirling about with a crown of flowers on her head, dancing beneath the guiding hand of the woman who'd placed it there. It was simple, it was beautiful, and it left him with a deep ache inside.

He would tell her. Tonight, he would tell her about Cordelia.

He shut his eyes against the vision, allowed the rays of the sun to warm his tired body, and drifted off to the sounds of happiness and laughter.

13

———

Murmurs of the men's voices and laughter came from the bunkhouse floating across on the refreshing breeze of the evening. The clucking of hens settling for the night, an occasional whinny of horses, even smells, once foreign, were now reassuring. In such a short time Madeline had come to love this rugged piece of land. For so long, she felt separate from the city she lived in, she now felt a part of this hidden piece of heaven on earth. It was easy to understand what brought men and their families to seek new lives out here. She had done the same, and it was bringing a steadiness to her heart and soul.

The rhythmic squeak of the rocking chairs only added to the peace of the night. Gideon was sitting silently next to her, having sent Tilly in to get ready for bed. Andrew was already upstairs in bed, but Madeline had a feeling that he was still sorting through his newfound pebbles and stones, by moonlight.

After an entertaining morning and a fun-filled afternoon by the creek, Madeline was enjoying the peace of the front porch. The seats of the chairs that she and Gideon now occupied were worn to a glossy smoothness from years of use, and she imagined Gideon's mother and father sitting here, as their children slept, proud of what they had built together in both family and land.

Even dinner tonight had had a different feeling. Gideon was attentive, and less reserved than he normally was, and the change was noticed by all those at the table. There were plenty of smiles and teasing taking place until the food appeared and full mouths and full bellies reduced the banter. Teresa had whipped up an especially large meal, as the boys were heading out to round up a band of horses from one of the pastures in the morning and would be gone for several days.

"It's going to be quiet here for a bit." Gideon continued to look out beyond the house.

Madeline laughed softly. "I'm not sure that's true. You've warned me yourself. It only takes one Hart to find some trouble."

He shot her a grin. "Fair enough."

Since he'd sent Tilly in, Gideon had had the look of a man who was mulling over something but wasn't quite ready to speak his mind. It was a beautiful evening, and the one thing Madeline had plenty of was time. So, she waited. If he wanted to say what was weighing on his mind, he would.

After a few minutes, he got up, leaned against the post, facing her.

"Madeline." He paused. "While I didn't like to hear what you and Andy went through, I appreciate that you trusted me enough to tell me."

"I'm sorry I didn't tell you sooner. I don't know why I didn't."

He waved away her apology. "Trust isn't easily given. I get that, and I'd be the last fella to fault you for it."

Madeline kept quiet. Gideon was still struggling with something.

"I know I've been acting real confusing. Hot and cold, so to speak."

"It's all right, Gideon. I understand."

"No, I don't think you do, which is why I need to tell you about Cordelia."

She watched him take off his hat and run his fingers through his thick hair; a nervous gesture she was beginning to recognize.

"I know it's not the same, but having lost my parents, I do know that a grieving heart takes time to heal. Some never do."

"No, it's not the same," said Gideon, "but not like you're thinking. I'm not grieving her, Madeline, I'm not even sure I ever did."

Her skin tingled with discomfort. This was the last thing she was expecting him to say. How was she supposed to respond to that?

"I know that sounds awful, but I need to tell you the truth. You need to know who I am if—well, you just need to know." He met her eyes, then looked away. "I couldn't make her happy. I tried. With all I had, I tried, but I couldn't do it. So, she found happiness elsewhere. With someone else."

"Gideon! I," she sputtered. "I don't understand."

"Her accident, the day she died, she was running away from me." He hesitated and looked toward the house behind her, then lowered his voice. "She was running away from Tilly too. She'd made it clear she wanted nothing to do with either one of us and she wasn't coming back."

Madeline's heart lurched. Was she hearing right? Was

Gideon saying that Cordelia willingly chose to leave them? She shook her head, as if it could sort his words into sense.

"She left her child? She left *Tilly*? How could—why?"

"I don't think Cordelia ever really wanted her, or children at all. I don't really know, and she wasn't interested in explaining." Gideon stood there struggling to keep eye contact with her.

"But Tilly? Her own flesh and blood, her child. I don't understand how anyone, any mother could do such a thing."

"Neither could I," said Gideon.

"And my sweet Tilly! She must be so hurt to know that her own mother could be so cruel. I don't know how she's remained such a sunny little girl."

Madeline thought her parent's failures, were painful, what this poor child must feel. To know her mother abandoned her. No wonder Gideon wasn't grieving the woman. Despite her tragic end, Madeline was hard-pressed to feel any sympathy for her.

"She doesn't know."

His words snapped her back from her harsh thoughts. "Pardon me?"

His voice still low, he explained. "I never told her. I never told anyone. Only Early knows, because he was there."

"Your brothers? Emma?"

"No."

"You never wanted to tell them?"

"I guess sometimes you tell a lie so long, you don't know how to stop, and one day it just becomes part of you. But that isn't the only lie."

She wanted to reassure him. "You can tell me anything."

Madeline couldn't imagine something worse than a mother abandoning her child for another man. Yet, she could see he was struggling, it was written all over his face, so she waited. Waited for him to let go of whatever had its hold on him.

"Tilly might not—Cordelia ... I don't even want to say the words. I never should have started talking."

"I'm here, Gideon."

His shoulders slumped and he released a long, slow breath. His brown eyes met hers, and he whispered. "Tilly might not be mine."

Nothing could have prepared her for those words. What Gideon was saying didn't make any sense. Tilly was a Hart, through and through.

"It's not true." She kept her voice low. The idea of Tilly overhearing her father's improbable doubts would never do.

"Cordelia said as much. Why would she lie about that?"

Madeline was incredulous. "*Why would she lie*? Can't you see? She wanted to hurt you. She wanted to leave a dark cloud over you, and she's done exactly that. Do you really believe that a woman who is willing to abandon her baby, would draw the line at lying to you? You can't believe that."

"I don't want to. More than anything, but there's this voice in my head, warning me to never let down my guard. That one day, she could be taken from me."

"She's yours, Gideon. I feel it in my heart. I wish you could see it all through my eyes."

"I wish I could too. But that's it. That's all of me; laid bare before you. Hoping it won't change the way you feel."

Madeline never expected the strong man before her could look so vulnerable. Her throat ached, and she was desperate to alleviate his obvious pain. She rose from the chair.

"I'm so sorry. No one should have to experience such heartache. I don't know what to say."

He shrugged one shoulder and put his hat back on. "Not much to say, really, things being the way they are. The way I'm hoping they could be. I thought you should know."

"Oh, Gideon." Madeline threw her arms around him, squeezing him so tightly, hoping he could feel the love she had, and know he didn't have to bear such pain alone. She wanted to take away the loneliness and the anguish he carried for so long.

At first, he stiffened. Then his muscles loosened, and he wrapped his strong arms around her, taking the comfort her body offered, into his. He held her there, in the warmth of his arms, accepting what she wanted to give him.

"Thank you," said Gideon.

She tilted her head up to look at him, and where she saw hurt, she also saw hope. She whispered, "You deserve to be loved, Gideon."

"Do I?" his voice was thick with emotion. A man desperate to know that he was worthy of kindness and affection. Desperate to know his heart didn't have to be locked away forever.

He lifted his fingers to her chin, and his thumb pressed against her bottom lip. As his thumb slipped away, he dipped his head.

"Daddy! I'm ready for my story!"

They tore apart, eyes wide, breath ragged, staring at each other. Her cheeks must have matched the fire she felt between them.

They stood there for a moment longer, only the night air and promise between them.

"Daddy?" The little voice called from inside the house.

Gideon grinned. "I thought you were teaching her not to yell."

"Thank goodness for my obvious failure," she replied with a smile.

He stared at her, and then brushed the back of his hand along her cheek. "Thank you."

Then he walked back into the house to find his daughter, leaving her alone on the porch, fingers touching her lips and trying to recover her breath. What would it have been like if he had actually kissed her?

It took several minutes before she gathered enough nerve to go inside the house. Madeline couldn't avoid Ben and Luke as they were playing an intense game of checkers on the small table by the floor-to-ceiling fireplace. Rhett was there too, reading the latest news sheets in a high-backed chair, that was turned in her direction.

All three men looked up as she entered, and Madeline was sure that the flush on her cheeks let them know what had taken place on the front porch.

Hooking a thumb toward Tilly's bedroom, Luke gave her a grin. "Gideon ran down that way."

"Oh, I think Tilly— her story—" she began to fumble over her words. Guilt was surely written all over her face.

Ben gave his brother a swift kick beneath the table.

Rhett cleared his throat. "I think I hear Andy calling upstairs."

Madeline shot Rhett a grateful look. "Thank you. I should go check on him. Good night."

"Certainly is," muttered Luke, then he let out a grunt as Ben kicked him again, much harder this time.

"Goodnight, Madeline," said Rhett.

Madeline nodded, not trusting herself to speak. If she'd suddenly grown wings, she could not have made it up the staircase any faster.

Replaying the events in her mind as she slipped into

bed, Madeline knew that despite the embarrassment with Gideon's brothers, this was the most wonderful night of her life. Still, with the men leaving early tomorrow, she would have a reprieve to compose herself and realize what all of this meant.

HE COULD STILL FEEL the soft skin of her neck beneath his fingers, and the softness of the lip his finger grazed. He hadn't meant to try and kiss her, that was the last thing on his mind when he started talking, but then she had thrown herself into his arms, and the love she offered flowed through to him, unshackling the chains from around his heart.

Taking a deep breath, he tried to shake the image of Madeline from his mind. He'd ignored the questioning faces of his brothers when he came in to read to Tilly, but that only gave him a brief respite. When he came back into the great room, they were waiting. If he had wagered on being able to go straight to bed, he would have lost.

"You must have really enjoyed the Sheriff's wedding to want another one so soon." Rhett didn't even look up from the papers he was reading as he spoke.

Luke snickered but gave Gideon a genuine smile. "I'm happy for you, and I'm also happy it's still not me."

Gideon turned to Ben. "Nothing from you?"

"Nope. I think Rhett covered it," said Ben. "I can't say I'm surprised, with the way you two been stepping around each other, but I am happy."

"And if I'm not sure where it's all headed?" he asked. Gideon thought he'd give his brothers a taste of their own medicine. He knew exactly what he wanted, and it was for

Madeline Sheppard to become his wife. "I mean, a man needs time to think about these things."

Luke leapt to his feet. "You wouldn't." He swung his head looking for support from Ben and Rhett. "I know you think I'm a little wild, but Madeline? She deser—"

Ben joined Luke, putting his hand on their young brother's shoulder. "Easy now, Luke. I'm sure Gideon realizes that should he not feel like doing the right thing by our Miss Madeline, then we'd all be happy to show him the error of his ways. If not, I'm not opposed to taking her to wife, myself."

Gideon stepped forward his eyes narrowed on Ben. He was about to give him a piece of his mind, when Rhett started laughing.

"Each one of you winding the other up, and not one of you smart enough to realize it. You boys have no idea how much I miss Micah and his level head."

The three of them glanced at Rhett, then turned back to each other, and started laughing.

Once they stopped and Ben and Luke were settled back at their game, Gideon thought it might be time to speak to his brothers about Cordelia too. If he was getting things off his chest, he might as well do it all at once.

He cleared his throat. "I wanted to tell you all something. I've told Madeline, because if she is willing to have me, I felt she needed to know."

All three gave him their attention and waited for him to talk.

"It's about Cordelia, and what happened. It wasn't good. We weren't good. She was leaving me on the day she died."

Gideon waited for the shock to appear on their faces, like it had on Madeline's, but the looks never came. They only glanced at each other and back to him.

Rhett spoke first. "We—I didn't know she was leaving, Gideon, but it was obvious that things weren't going well. We're your family, we knew, but you needed time to work through whatever it was you were feeling."

"Why didn't you say anything?" asked Gideon.

"We did," reminded Ben. "If you recall, you weren't real open to hashing it out. Guess we figured you'd come find us when you were ready to talk. And it looks like you have."

Gideon dropped his head, shaking it, before he looked up. "I don't want Tilly to know."

"Nothing to know," assured Luke. Ben and Rhett nodded.

Gideon thought back to what Madeline had said about his family. That he didn't know how lucky he was to have the bond he did with his siblings. She was right. When you're blessed everyday with something, it can easily be taken for granted.

"Since it's not me, I'm glad you've found a good woman, Gideon. For you and Tilly," said Luke. "I gotta tell you, I knew last night, watching you two dancing that she was the one."

Ben scoffed. "Then you're blind as a bat."

"If you're so smart, when did you know?" demanded Luke.

"Day he brought that little mustang home. Gideon said it was just for Andy, but it was Madeline's smile he was watching the whole time." Ben jumped two of Luke's checkers. "I'm always ahead of you, kid."

Rhett rolled his eyes and went back to reading, and Gideon squeezed Ben's shoulder as he left them to their game.

Heading to his room, he felt lighter than he had in years.

14

The morning had been hot and dry, and with the men gone out to switch pastures for the horses, the air around the ranch was almost silent. Madeline realized she'd grown used to the sounds of gates opening and closing, shovels scraping along old wooden boards, and the shouts in the yard. Without them, the ranch seemed almost empty.

Stink was still here. He'd sent them off with enough food supplies to get them through the few days they were gone. Billy McCarty and a couple other men stayed behind to tend to chores and stock. Tilly was enjoying the chance to teach Madeline about milking cows and the hazards of collecting eggs. Andrew spent as much time as possible with Luna, and the moment he was finished with lessons, he was back out to rub her down, or simply sit and chat with her.

Madeline was happy, the children were happy, and it was Gideon she had to thank for it all. From the moment he agreed, under duress from his sister, to take them in, to the last night's events on the porch, he'd made both Andrew's and her life richer. The idea that she might become a mother to Tilly filled her with a love that could not have been greater than if the little girl had been her own. As for Andrew, it was a good thing that they would be staying at the Double H. Madeline doubted she'd have been able to drag him away.

Ignoring the smiles on the Hart boys' faces, Madeline had gotten up early on the morning they left, so that she could say goodbye to Gideon. She was glad she had, as he gave her a quick hug, and whispered that he had something to ask her when he got back. Everything was falling so perfectly in place; Madeline couldn't believe the wonderful turn their lives had taken.

She still hadn't heard anything from her father's barrister. At this point, she didn't really care if she ever did. The next time she was in town, she planned on sending another note, letting her Uncle August know that if he agreed to leave her and Andrew alone, to live their lives in Autumns Springs, she would relinquish all claims to her family's money. Some might argue that he didn't deserve it, and they'd be right, but Madeline much preferred being safe and happy to right. She'd discovered a world of riches that no amount of money could buy, and she wouldn't allow anything to jeopardize that.

"You certainly have a spring in your step today."

Teresa stood from where they were weeding around the carrots and wiping her hands on her apron as she smiled at Madeline.

Taking a deep breath of fresh air, Madeline looked to the sky. "It is an exceptionally beautiful day, is it not?"

"Of course, of course. And nothing to do with the fact the boys are returning today?" teased Teresa.

"Oh, is that today?" grinned Madeline.

Teresa laughed and waved her away.

Madeline glanced over to where Tilly and Andrew were absorbed in a game of marbles, belly first in the dirt. At one time, she might have fretted over Tilly's clothes, but they were finding a balance, between what was acceptable for life on a ranch and life in the city. Earlier, the little girl had tried convincing Andrew to play Cat's Cradle, but he wasn't having any of it. Even the fact that her brother was comfortable speaking his mind so openly now was wonderful. Tilly, of course, took his rejection of her suggestion in stride, and quickly came up with the idea of marbles. The tableau of the two children landed in her heart and warmed her soul.

Once they finished in the garden, Madeline packed up a basket filled with Teresa's baking, and she took Tilly and Andrew back down to the creek. She needed to keep herself busy. If she stayed around the house, she'd spend more time looking out for Gideon's return than keeping an eye on the children.

The plan was to go into Autumn Springs for supper at Nora and Micah's, once the men returned. Madeline didn't know how they would stay upright after that much riding, but the Hart boys didn't seem fazed by the idea at all. Still, she hoped they returned sooner rather than later.

Busy making rafts from twigs, twine, and leaves for sails, Madeline didn't see the small party of men approaching, until she heard the pounding of hooves. Thinking it must be the Harts arriving back early, she spun around with a friendly smile.

Then froze.

"Miss Sheppard. How nice to receive such a welcoming smile."

Reuben Snook: handsome, fast-talking, son of the devil, and her Uncle August's right hand man. His six men stayed back on their mounts, but he rode closer.

"Mr. Snook."

"Ah, you haven't forgotten me. You should know how much that pleases me. It feels like you've been gone an eternity, and here you are, flattering me with your remembrances."

His tone was congenial, but Madeline had enough experience to know that beneath the pleasant exterior was a brute who delighted in others' misfortunes. His saccharine smile was only a mask to cover his scheming black heart. She needed to walk a fine line with Snook. His temper was quick, she was alone, and she the only one between him and the children. His timing was too convenient. Had he been watching them? He must have known that Gideon and his brothers were away.

"How could I forget?" Madeline walked toward him a few steps, then stopped, hoping to draw his attention away from Tilly and Andrew. "How did you find us?"

"You have yourself to thank for that, Miss Sheppard. I must say, you're an excellent dancer." He swept off his hat, then settled it back on with a wink. "Your telegram was much appreciated. You let us know exactly where you were, which was most helpful. Just when I started to worry I wouldn't find you."

The telegram! "How did—"

"Come now, your uncle is a well-connected man, surely you can see that. The lawyer certainly did."

The barrister had betrayed her confidence. And for what? A few extra coins to jingle in his pockets. Her father may have trusted the man, but she was a fool to have done the same.

"What do you want from me, Mr. Snook?"

He gave her a leering gaze. "Such an open question, my

dear! For now, I only wish to bring you back to where you belong."

Several of the distasteful men behind him snickered at the insolent remark. Madeline knew she was in a lot of trouble if she didn't handle this correctly. She turned to check on the children and saw they had stopped playing and were watching the scene unfolding before them. Tilly looked nervous and reached for Andrew's hand. Andrew looked terrified and Madeline wanted to weep.

"I see your brother there too. And what a lovely girl with him," said Snook. "That's a mighty swift river there. Are you sure that you being here is safe for those children? I would hate to see anything happen to them."

It was a barely a stream, and they both knew it, but Snook was making his message clear. If she wanted to keep the children safe, she was going to have to play along. Causing any trouble for him would mean trouble for the children.

"I understand."

"Good."

Madeline couldn't let anything happen to them. Gideon would never forgive her if something happened to Tilly because of her. She wouldn't be able to forgive herself either. She didn't think these men would be foolish enough to harm the little girl without cause. That would be inviting a mess they didn't need. So, the best thing to do, was give them no cause to do so. But she also had Andrew to worry about. She wasn't willing to put him in danger either, not after they'd made it so far.

"Mr. Snook," Madeline took a deep breath and straightened her shoulders as she approached his horse, looked up into the soulless man's eyes and lowered her voice. "I'll come with you, without argument or trouble, but please, let me leave my brother here. Andrew is of no use to you."

Snook leaned down. "You got that useless part right. Are you trying to negotiate with me, Miss Sheppard? I don't think you're in much of a position to do so."

A shiver ran through her, at his cruel sneer. "No. I'm only saying that he's not part of this, my father's will. Leaving him here is your easiest option."

Snook slid off his horse and ran a finger from her shoulder down to her arm. "What's in it for me?"

Of course, the man never did anything he wasn't paid for in some way or another. Her cheeks flamed at the humiliation, and she squeezed her eyes against the threatening tears.

"Aw, you don't have to answer, Miss Sheppard. I'll think of something."

The blood in her veins turned ice cold. There was not end to the depths of this man's depravity. Not that any of it mattered. She would do whatever it took to save Andrew and Tilly. But first, she needed to get these men away from the children.

"Please." She heard the fear in her voice, and knew Snook heard it too. It seemed to please him.

He gazed past her to the children with disgust. "He'd only slow us down. We'll leave him behind."

"Thank you. May I say goodbye to them?"

Pleased he had frightened her, and that she wasn't putting up a fight, he agreed. "Be quick about it."

Hiding her panic with a false smile, she walked back down to the children.

"What's going on?" whispered Tilly.

"Don't leave, Maddie. Please," begged Andrew, his voice barely audible.

"I have to. You'll be okay. The Harts will take good care of you. Be good. I'll be back, I promise." She hugged him, her heart aching at the confusion in his face.

"Let's go, Miss Sheppard," called Snook, his patience was at an end.

Tilly let go of Andrew's hand and threw her arms around Madeline's waist. "Please don't. I wanted you to be my momma, but now you're going too."

The little girl's pleas pierced her core. Words she once longed to hear, now ripped at her heart.

"Miss Sheppard." Snook's mount reacted to the warning in his voice and pawed at the ground.

Madeline peeled Tilly's tight grip from her body, and then she stepped away. If Tilly started making a fuss, it would only make things worse. She couldn't let that happen.

"I love you both, so much. I'm so sorry to leave like this, but it's for the best. Please, look after each other. Go straight home. Do you hear me? Straight home."

"Maddie?" Andrew's quivering voice, almost broke her, but then resolve kicked in.

"I want to go, Andrew. This is my choice. It's better for you here." Her icy tone drew a gasp from both children, but Madeline didn't turn around, she couldn't, not yet.

She walked quickly back to Snook, grabbing her shawl from the blanket on the way. She didn't want to anger him further, so allowed him to place her on his horse. Then he jumped up behind her.

"Now, isn't this nice?"

Her stomach turned as he spoke, his arms wrapped around her, keeping her still. She looked back to see Andrew and Tilly clinging to each other at the water's edge. They were devastated, but they were safe, and that was all that mattered.

THE LAST THREE miles felt like an eternity. All Gideon wanted to do was get back to the Double H and to Madeline. The boys had been teasing him for the last two days, but he didn't care. He was headed home, and he was going to ask Madeline to marry him.

Ever since that night on the porch when he shared the truth, and that near kiss with her, Madeline Sheppard was all he could think about. The moment she told him he deserved love too, he felt like he'd stepped back into the light.

Gideon couldn't wait to share the news with Tilly. She'd never had a mother, not really, and he knew that she would be as excited as he was to start this new path in their lives. If things went as well as he hoped, he and Madeline could announce their intentions to marry when they were at Micah's.

Picturing his sister's face, Gideon smiled. Emma would be tickled pink to know her plan worked so well. He didn't mind. He was mighty happy it was working out too. Maybe, God willing, in a year's time, they would have a little one too. A playmate for Emma and Wes's new addition.

Gideon chuckled. He was getting way ahead of himself. He still had to get Madeline to agree to be his wife, but he was thinking the odds were in his favor. How his brothers felt the need to remind him that he needed to do right by her was almost comical now. He wasn't the sort to play with another's emotions. What they shared was more than a fleeting desire. It was a promise, a promise he intended to keep.

When the main house, and the outbuildings of the

Double H began to appear in the distance, Gideon gave his horse its head, and a gentle kick of encouragement.

"Oh sure, now you're not tired!" Luke called to his back.

He heard his brothers laughing behind him, but he knew they understood his hurry. They were all happy for him too.

When he got to the house, Teresa and Mendo were on the porch waiting. He threw the reins over the post and took the stairs two at a time.

He greeted Teresa with a kiss on her cheek. "Where are they?"

"Gideon ..." Teresa eyes welled up with tears.

Mendo stepped forward. "Miss Madeline is gone."

"What?" Gideon shook his head at the words. He couldn't have that heard right. Through the buzzing that started in his ears, he heard himself speak., "What do you mean 'gone'?"

He grabbed Mendo's shoulders and started shaking them. "What do you mean?"

He could hear the pounding of hooves as his brothers arrived, but he never took his eyes from his foreman.

"I don't know, Gideon. Tilly and Andy came back from the river without her. They were all tears, and fit to be tied, but all I could get out of them was that she left with some man."

"Some man? Did she leave or was she taken?"

Mendo shrugged. "They said she went willingly. She told Andy that he couldn't come, he had to stay here."

"What's going on?" Ben joined Gideon on the porch.

"She left," replied Gideon. He felt like one of those inflated balloons, that was losing its air. "With a man."

"What? That doesn't make any sense," argued Ben. "She wouldn't just leave."

Well, she did," spit Gideon. "And she left Andy here, with us."

Gideon glared at his brother. Couldn't Ben see what was right in front of him? It was happening again. History was repeating itself.

The rocking chair he'd sat in next to Madeline, only days before, mocked him. Gideon kicked at it. Luke and Rhett came up the stairs but said nothing.

Ben frowned. "No. This isn't right."

"You don't have to tell me," said Gideon. His skin was cold and hot at the same time. He was having a hard time putting together his thoughts. "I need to talk to Tilly and Andy."

"Who would she leave with, Gid? Who did she say she sent that telegram too?"

Telegram?

"What telegram? When? Why is this the first time I'm hearing this?" Anger crept into his voice.

"I didn't know it mattered," Ben looked to Luke and Rhett for back up.

Luke shook his head and Rhett shrugged, his hands up. Guess they didn't know about it either, but Ben did. Why the blazes didn't he say something?

"She sent it on the day I took her to town." Ben looked confused. "I mean, she was a little funny about it, but I didn't think anything of it."

Madeline sure didn't say a word about sending a message to anyone. She told him that her uncle didn't know where she was, and that was after she apparently sent this telegram. Was there someone else? Why hadn't she told him she sent a message? What was she hiding from him?

Gideon swore, and strode past the LaBaenas, leaving his brothers on the porch.

"Tilly! Andy!" He was hollering for the children, when he heard Bandit bark from Tilly's bedroom.

When he opened the door, Tilly and Andy were sitting on the floor, looking like two sad lost souls, Bandit snuggled between them. Gideon's heart tore in two.

"She's gone, Daddy." Tilly got up and threw her sobbing body into his. Andy just sat there, running his fingers through the patches of white and black of Bandit's hair. He didn't even look up.

"We asked her to stay, but she wouldn't. She said we had to look after each other now, and that it was for the best." Tilly took another shaky breath. "Why'd she do that, Daddy?"

Gideon didn't have an answer for his daughter, least not one with words for children's ears. This moment reminded him why he had never told Tilly the truth about her mother. She would be devastated if she knew.

"Who did she leave with?" He was still finding it hard to believe she left willingly. How could he have been so wrong, again?

"A man, and his friends. They came to the river on horses."

"Have you ever seen them before."

"No," sniffed Tilly.

Tilly's tears subsided enough to tell him as much as she remembered. Andy still wasn't talking. Gideon didn't blame the poor kid. He couldn't imagine how he'd be feeling if his siblings abandoned him.

"He was touching her arm, and he said he was worried he'd never see her again, and he said thank you for sending the telegram."

Every word was like a dagger through his heart, cutting off pieces that would never be put back together. He should be glad she wasn't hurt, taken from them, but somehow knowing she'd left of her own free will felt just as bad.

Ben may not believe it, but Ben only saw the good in people, he couldn't comprehend Madeline doing such a thing. Gideon knew better, yet he'd made the same mistake. Andy may not be her son, but he was family and she'd abandoned him, just like Cordelia.

And yet. What if he was wrong? What if the children weren't remembering things right? He needed to be sure.

"Are you sure she wanted to go with this man, Tilly? Andy? Real sure?"

"Yes, Daddy. She looked like you when you're all done with Uncle Luke. She said I want to go, it's my choice. She went on his horse, and he was hugging her."

Gideon glanced at Andrew, who looked up long enough to nod in agreement with Tilly. Blazes! It was unlikely they were both wrong, and Tilly was clear about what Madeline said. If there was any shred of hope he was wrong, it was now gone.

Why had she even bothered to pretend she cared? Did she think she wouldn't be able to reunite with this man and settled for him, the man who would provide without question for her and her brother?

He wanted to ride after her. Demand an explanation, tell her not to go, to give them a chance, that he loved her, and he'd do anything to make her happy. But he'd already done that once before. It was a mistake then, and it would be a mistake now. No one can be forced to love another, and only a fool would try.

He sighed, as he held Tilly. Using his other arm, he pulled Andy against his body. It was hard to see what the future might hold for them, but he'd been through it before, and he could get through it again.

"We'll be okay," he whispered as he held them. "You got us, Andy, and we got you. You'll always have a home here."

GIDEON SPENT the rest of the afternoon with Tilly and Andy, trying to settle them down. He decided after a day like this, it would be best if they both stayed at the Double H instead of going into town.

His brothers met him in the office, still thinking there was some misunderstanding. When Gideon told them what Tilly said, they stopped questioning him. But their words got him to thinking. His brothers, Emma, Nora, the whole town seemed to approve of her. If Madeline was only pretending this whole time, she was the best liar he'd ever met.

It wasn't only the moment they shared, it was the way she'd comforted him, when he told her about Cordelia. The way she looked at him, as they danced at the Wyley's wedding. And even if she didn't feel the same way he did, what about Tilly? Watching her with his daughter, Madeline was attentive and loving. Cordelia couldn't even put that much effort into a child that was her own. And Andy. The woman he knew was ready to knock him nine ways from Sunday, just for getting her brother atop a horse. How could a woman so worried about something as simple as that, leave her brother behind? After everything she'd told him it didn't make sense.

Madeline accused him of making assumptions all the time. He knew that the experience with Cordelia had soured him, and made him quick to believe the worst, instead of giving people a chance. If he was doing that now, and Madeline was in danger and needed him, then he'd never forgive himself.

He needed to talk to Emma, or Nora. If they were with her when she sent that telegram, maybe it would shed some light on the situation. They might know something, anything.

Gideon knew he would sound like a desperate man, and maybe he'd be the laughingstock of town, but while his mind was advising caution, his heart was refusing to let go.

15

———

With every mile from the Double H, Madeline pictured Andrew and Tilly safe, and it helped to reinforce her courage. It was the hardest thing she'd had to do, when she walked away from them after being so cold, but she'd had no choice. Protecting them was all that mattered, and knowing Tilly the way she did, she didn't want the outspoken girl to cause a scene. Tilly had never dealt with men like this, she only knew the love of her family, and the kindness of the Double H staff. The little girl couldn't understand the danger they'd be in, if Madeline put up a fight. She needed to make it believable she was going willingly.

She tried to explain to Snook, that she wasn't going to fight her uncle. That she was going to sign off on everything. All he had to do was take her into Autumn Springs, where the paperwork could be drawn up. He only laughed at her, letting her know that her uncle was taking what he needed, and whether she agreed or not made no difference for him.

The way he was talking, Madeline started to question why the awful man didn't kill her outright. Her uncle would have no one to contest his claim, and Snook wouldn't need to bring her back. She didn't know whether to count herself lucky, or to fear what her uncle planned for her. Madeline tried to calm herself with the belief that as soon as Uncle August knew she didn't want the money, that he could have it all in exchange for her freedom, he would let her go. It was the easiest solution for all of them. It had to work.

The pace their party was kept was relentless. Madeline overheard he was trying to make Butte, and get on the train that would get them to Portland before anyone took it in their heads to come after them.

But Snook's single-mindedness was his own undoing. He refused to stop at any stage stations to switch out their horses, and the poor exhausted creatures slowed down so much, that by the time Snook reached the station, the last train of the day had already left. Curse as he might, they had no option but to stay in the city overnight.

The next day, Madeline's eyes were heavy from the sleepless night she'd spent at the hotel, two of Snook's men standing guard outside her door. They were the same two apes on either side of her now, as she stood on the platform, waiting for the early morning train. Other than Snook, who'd gone off in search of food, they were the last of the men who had taken her from the Double H. The others, hired guns in case of trouble, were paid the night before and had already left.

The white-haired ticket agent walked by for the second time. His concern for her was evident, but seeing the company she was keeping, he didn't stop. She gave him a brave smile as he passed. Madeline didn't want the elderly man to be needlessly hurt on her behalf. Shuffling back to his office, he watched her from his window between ticket sales.

Self-consciously adjusting the simple skirts she had on, Madeline felt completely out of her element. She pulled her shawl tightly across her chest, then folded her arms in her lap. The two men stopped trying to speak to her a while ago, as she was refusing to acknowledge them at all. They'd taken to calling her Miss High-and-Mighty, but their words meant nothing. She wasn't going engage with the despicable men.

As she waited, her thoughts turned to Gideon. If the children believed her, then when they told Gideon, he would feel absolutely betrayed. Madeline knew how similar her leaving might feel to him, after all he had been through. There was no way to help it, but that didn't ease her guilt. If only she could get a message to him, letting him know why she'd left, and that she loved him, and would return the moment she was able.

She glanced over to the ticket agent. Maybe there was a way.

The moment she stood, the two men at her side jumped up.

"Where ya headed, Miss High 'n Mighty?" smirked one. "Snook told you to stay put."

"Mr. Snook didn't say I couldn't stretch my legs." She gave the man a long assessing glare. "Are you afraid you can't defend yourself against a woman?"

"I ain't afraid of nothin'," said the man. "Walk if you want, but you ain't walking alone."

Turning up her chin, she didn't bother to respond, instead making her way slowly to the ticket booth. As she got closer, the agent became wide-eyed. If she was to pull this off, she was going to require him to be far more subtle. His fearful appraisal of the men at her side were dashing her hopes.

Before she could speak, a loud booming crash and screams funneled down the platform. The agent pushed his head out his window to get a better look at the ruckus, and the men at her side tried peering around the people swarming to get a better look.

"What in the—?"

"Fight! Fight!" The crowd yelled.

It sounded like there was a whole group of men brawling, but with everyone running to watch, it was impossible to see.

"I'm going," said the one man next to her.

"Aw, I want to see too," whined the other one.

Gasps of horror and delight emanated from the crowd as the fight continued.

The two men began to argue, like Tweedle-dum and Tweedle-dee from the "Original Ditties for the Nursery" book she used to read as a little girl. Madeline was about to use their bickering to signal to the ticket agent, when they turned on her.

"Stay right here. Don't ya move, or you'll regret it, Missy." They must have thought she was sufficiently threatened, as they both left to watch the battle taking place inside the crowd.

Immediately Madeline turned to the elderly man behind the glass.

"Sir, please can you help me?"

The man's eyes bulged, but he wasn't looking at her. Madeline was turning to look behind her, when a huge hand clamped over her mouth, and she was dragged toward the ticket office.

She couldn't see her attacker, but the agent looked terrified as the door to his office was kicked open. She bit down on the hand that covered her mouth, and heard a yelp, as she was spun around.

"Gideon!"

He wasn't alone. Pastor Woods was there too. The poor disheveled preacher had his back against the door, holding it tight, and looking completely bewildered. Madeline didn't know why he'd chosen the Pastor to help him rescue her, when he had so many brothers.

The old man tried to sidle away, but Gideon took one step toward him, and he put his hands up.

"You stay at the window," said Gideon.

The ticket agent nodded. "Fine, fine. I didn't like the looks of those other fellers much, anyway."

"Madeline!" Gideon ran his eyes across her body, looking for any obvious injury. Then he took her in his arms.

She started to weep. She'd been so frightened, but in Gideon's embrace, she was safe. She should have told him why her uncle might search for her. Why hadn't she?

"I'm so sorry—"

"We don't have a lot of time." He thrust her back, his hands gripping her arms tightly. "Do you love me?"

"What?"

He looked like he wanted to shake her. "I need to know if you love me, Madeline."

"Of course, I do. Hasn't it been obvious?" She didn't understand.

"I need you to say it."

"Say it?"

"Woman, we don't have time to be repeating every word I say. Just answer the question. Tell me true." He sucked the air in through his teeth. "Do. You. Love. Me?"

It was then that she saw how deeply this big, strong man

had been hurt. His voice was with choked with emotion, and his eyes begging and his urgency tangible. Madeline knew she was going to do everything in her power to push away that pain. She wouldn't keep him waiting.

"Yes. Yes, I love you! Every brooding, assuming, sweet, protective inch of you. From the moment I saw you in town with Tilly, I knew you were different. You were so kind to Andrew, and to me. I never thought there would be room in your heart, but the day out on the porch, when you were consoling Andrew, it didn't even matter, I knew I could never love another. Then at the dance—"

"Madeline Sheppard. I love every word you're saying, but I need you to stop talking and answer one more question."

Heavy footsteps pounded on the platform boards, in their direction.

"She's gone! You idiots. You're lucky I don't kill you both, here and now. Keep looking."

Pastor Woods ducked down, and Gideon looked to the agent who nodded and casually took his usual place at the window. Then he pulled her down with him, next to the pastor.

"Marry me. Be my wife."

The sweet hopeful look in his eyes, almost made her shout her response, then she whispered. "Yes. Yes, I want nothing more."

"Good, because we aren't waiting." smiled Gideon, then he elbowed the preacher. "Your turn."

Pastor Woods was white as a ghost as he pulled his bible from his coat pocket. He cleared his throat and prepared to begin.

"Just what's needed Pastor, we don't have a lot of time here," reminded Gideon.

"Right," said the pastor.

He leaned in and quietly asked both her and Gideon if they agreed to take each other in holy matrimony. 'I do's' were quickly spoken, and he declared them husband and wife. There was no time to kiss the bride, as the office door burst open.

Gideon jumped to his feet, gun drawn, as he stepped in front of Madeline as she and the Pastor straightened up.

Snook didn't move, his own pistol pointed at Gideon's belly.

"Oh, dear, oh dear," stammered the ticket agent.

"Looks like we're at an impasse," said Snook. "But I'm going to wager that you're not the killing kind, so if I were you, I'd step to the side, cowboy." Behind him, the two ruffians arrived, scowls on their faces, and guns in their hands.

Gideon didn't move an inch. "I don't recall inviting these gentlemen to our wedding, do you, Mrs. Hart?"

Madeline didn't answer. They were outnumbered, and she was terrified that Snook wouldn't back down.

"Married? I don't believe it. There was no time." Snook eyes darted to the preacher, then back to Gideon.

"Ask the pastor," said Gideon.

Pastor Woods swallowed then nodded. "It's true. Declaration and Pronouncement."

"Even got ourselves a witness." Gideon indicated to the poor ticket agent who was probably wishing he hadn't come to work today.

"You won't get away with this," Snook said, as he cocked the hammer on his gun.

Madeline held her breath, with the ominous click. The barrel was pointed at Gideon, and if fired, there was no room to escape. Would Snook be foolish enough, angry enough to shoot?

"Any gun that noisy, sounds like something you should be fixing, not pointing." Gideon shook his head. "And you may want to look behind you."

Snook didn't turn but his two men did, and realized they were surrounded. Through the door, Madeline saw Weston, Rhett, Ben, Luke and Micah. They were all looking tussled and a little worse for wear, but grimly ready to put an end to this spectacle. They must have created quite the diversion so that Gideon could reach her.

The two men quickly holstered their guns, but Snook took a moment before he did the same.

"This isn't over. Once Mr. Sheppard finds out what you've pulled here, there's going to be trouble. The kind that you've never seen, cowboy." Snook's threat didn't even seem to convince himself.

"I think that if he's a smart businessman, he'll move on."

"And why's that?" sneered Snook.

"Well, if he likes doing business anywhere in Oregon, then he should know what a good friend Zenas Moody was of my father's. They go way back to when Governor Moody was still moving wool with the Oregon and Montana Transportation Company. Smart man would want to stay on the governor's good side."

Madeline almost choked. The Harts knew the governor of Oregon? She knew that they ran a big operation, but she never even considered how far their influence reached.

"Gideon, is that true?"

"Yes, ma'am. There's a lot you don't know about us Harts, but I plan on spending the rest of my life telling you all about it."

"Get them outta here, boys."

Snook shook off Rhett's hold on him, and lifted his chin, with a contemptuous smile.

"There won't be charges, she came willingly." Snook's mocking eyes met hers. "Isn't that right, sweetheart?"

"We'll see about that," replied Gideon.

Weston and the Hart brothers unceremoniously hauled Snook and his men away from the office. Gideon turned around, folding Madeline into his arms. She never wanted him to let go of her. This is where she felt safe, she felt loved.

"Hold on, boys," Gideon said, releasing her. Walking over to the fuming Snook, he sidestepped the stream of spit aimed for his boot.

"Forgive me, Pastor." Glancing briefly at Madeline, he pulled back and put his fist straight into Snook's mouth. The shocked man grunted in pain.

Gideon growled. "That's for touching my wife."

EPILOGUE

The day was perfect.

The first breath of air this morning had been cool and crisp, a reminder that fall would soon be here, but the sun lifted once again in a clear blue sky that shone above the gathering.

The entire Hart family was together for a picnic, knowing the final days of summer were upon them.

Madeline watched Tilly and Andrew playing Blind Man's Bluff with Luke, Micah and Nora.

Weston was sitting on one of the blankets spread out on the grass away from the creek, with his new daughter in his arms. Ben, Rhett, and Gideon took turns making faces at the baby, each hoping to be the first to coax a smile.

"Quite a scene, isn't it?"

Emma came up from behind Madeline, wrapping one arm around Madeline's waist. She squeezed Emma's hand, and then they sat down on another blanket, leaving the men to their activities.

They sat quietly enjoying the view until Madeline broke their silence.

"Thank you, Emma."

Emma smiled. "For what?"

"All of this. Everything before us. For what you did for us, when we first got off that stage in Autumn Springs. I don't know if I ever really said how grateful I am."

The normally forthright Emma blushed. "I think it's Bandit we should all be thanking."

"You know what I mean," said Madeline, shaking her head at her sister-law. "You changed my life. Andrew's life."

"And you changed ours," said Emma. "I'm happy to take all the credit for getting you to the Double H, but as the saying goes 'you can lead a horse to water, but you can't make it drink. In this case the horse is a stubborn Hart."

"Those last words are very true," laughed Madeline.

At the sound of their merriment, Gideon looked across to meet Madeline's gaze and gave her a slow satisfied smile. One glance from her husband still warmed her to her toes.

Husband. It was still hard to believe she was married.

Only last week, she had received a telegram from both Uncle August and her father's barrister. The unscrupulous lawyer had let her know that with her marriage, the entirety of her inheritance would be transferred, to an institution of her own choice. The shameless man even offered to continue his work for her family. Her response to his message took few words.

It was that same day word came from her uncle letting her know that he wished Madeline and her new husband well. He also apologized for any misunderstanding she might have had regarding his intentions as their guardian. He professed that he'd only sent his men to ensure her safety, as she had left Portland so quickly. When she read the letter to Gideon, he didn't seem shocked at all.

"Men like your uncle only care about one thing: themselves. What you're holding there is another form of self-preservation. Snook must have told him of our connection to Governor Moody. No businessman wants the governor of any state as his enemy."

He was right, of course, and Madeline accepted the letter for what it was, and chose not to respond.

Having seen Gideon with Tilly, and watching him now with his new niece, Madeline hoped that in time, they might be sitting here together with a little one of their own. She had so much to be grateful for.

She watched now with amusement as the poor men began to panic. Lusty wails had started up from the blanketed babe, and all four of them called to Emma for help.

Laughing, Emma got up from the blanket, and went over to grab her daughter. "You've all done very well, but there are some things even you boys can't do."

The Harts all wrinkled their faces in discomfort, while Weston only sighed with relief as he passed Mabel up.

As Emma lifted her, one of her blankets fell away, revealing a pair of wiggling bare legs.

Gideon let out an odd sound, causing everyone to look his way. "Her leg. She—."

"That?" Emma brushed a finger across the heart-shaped mark on the baby's leg. Scooping up the blanket and tucking back around her daughter, she replied. "It's a birthmark, Gideon, she's fine. It's just like the one Mama had."

Emma kissed the soft tufts atop Mabel's head. "I think it's nice to know that in some visible way, we are still connected to her. In mind and body."

As Madeline approached, she could see the thoughts racing through Gideon's mind, as easily if he had spoken them.

"What do you mean, 'like Mama'?" He was trying to

keep his tone light, but Madeline knew he was struggling. "I never saw it." He looked to his brothers, "Any of you know this?"

Rhett shrugged, then Ben said, "You, okay? I don't remember, Gid, but I think it's nice that she's got a little piece of Mama, tattooed right on her."

Gideon jumped up. "Are you sure? I never saw it."

"Oh, for heaven's sake, why would you? It's not like Mama was walking around showing her legs, Gideon." Emma shook her head. "I know she had one, because I was sad that I didn't have such pretty heart on me. She said it skips a generation. Her mother didn't have it, but her grandmother did. So, now Mabel has it."

"That's wonderful," said Gideon, his eyes shining. "Tilly —Tilly has one too."

"Makes sense, she's Mama's granddaughter too. It nice to know both girls have it. A blessing really."

"A blessing indeed," agreed Gideon, then he started to laugh.

"Honestly Gideon, I don't know what gets into you sometimes. Now, if you'll excuse me, I need to take care of this little miss," said Emma, then she went and found a shady spot beneath a tree.

Madeline looked at Gideon. She could see he was near tears, and if he didn't want to do any explaining, she needed to act fast.

Madeline held out her hand. "Gideon, would you mind taking a walk with me? There are some things I'd like to gather for one of the children's lessons."

Gideon stopped laughing but he was still grinning when he nodded and took her arm in his.

His grip was tight, as though he were trying to keep himself controlled until they moment they were out of sight.

Then he lifted her up and spun her around. "She's mine. She's mine, Madeline! She's mine."

He was trying to keep his voice low, but his excitement was palpable as he set her back on the ground. In a single moment, years of worry and fear washed away. Madeline was brimming with happiness for him. It had always been clear in her heart, that Tilly was his daughter. If not by blood, then in all the ways that really mattered.

"She's always been your daughter, but I'm glad that you can now believe it too."

"My love for her doesn't change, I can't love her more than I already do. But she's mine, which means she can never be taken from me, from us. I can breathe, our family is safe."

Madeline placed her palm on his cheek. "We are."

Gideon let out a deep breath, enfolding her in his arms. As they stayed in each other's embrace, his racing heart finally slowed down,

Deciding to walk back to the clearing before someone came looking for them, Madeline and Gideon returned to their family. Gideon ran to join Tilly and the others in their game, and he looked like a younger man. Years of worry and fear had lifted from his soul, allowing him to truly breathe again. Even Luke looked surprised to see his eldest brother enjoying himself with such enthusiasm.

Madeline watched as Gideon scooped up Tilly and hugged her tightly when he caught her. With his daughter's face tucked into his shoulder he looked across at her and mouthed the words 'I love you'.

Emma came up from behind her and handed Madeline the newest addition to the family. "He really does, you know. Yet, I still haven't received a thank you from him for my efforts. One would think the man would be more grateful."

Kissing the downy head of the newborn, Madeline softly laughed. "Good luck with that."

Emma waved a hand. "It's fine. I'm sure Ben, at least, will be grateful when I offer to help him find a wife. He'd make a wonderful husband and father, don't you think?"

Shaking her head, Madeline grinned. "I think that Ben is going to be very thankful he's leaving soon for his trip into the city. He might even extend it, if he knows what you have planned for him back at home."

"There's a few new women in town, one of them may be just what Ben needs." Emma looked briefly pensive.

Madeline shrugged. "Who knows, maybe the perfect woman is waiting for him in Butte."

"Can you imagine?" Emma laughed. "No, there is absolutely no chance. He's on serious business. He's taking care of some ranch business but the thing he's excited about is the thoroughbred he so desperately wants. He's finally purchased the horse and will be picking it up on his way back through Butte."

"All that excitement for one horse?" Madeline was amazed, until she remembered how much Andrew loved Luna.

"Yes, one horse." Emma shook her head. "I don't understand it either, but this dream of his is all he thinks and talks about. The perfect stable of horses."

"It must be a very special horse," said Madeline.

"A very expensive horse." Emma sighed. "Yet, he won't take a penny from the ranch. It's taken him years to save the money. Stubborn man wants to prove he's bringing something of his own to the table. Typical Hart. Right now he has a one track mind. Even if the perfect woman fell right into his lap, he would never notice."

"You sound quite certain," remarked Madeline, amused by Emma's confident statement.

Emma smiled. "Trust me. Unless she has four legs and a tail, Ben wouldn't even know she was there."

WILL Ben make it back to the Double H without a bride? Grab your copy of **BEN'S GAMBLE** to find out!

www.ingramcontent.com/pod-product-compliance
Lightning Source LLC
Chambersburg PA
CBHW072008210726
48294CB00013B/1721